There Was an Old Woman

by

June Summers

There Was an Old Woman

Cover Art by *Kristian Norris*

The Wild Rose Press, Inc.
PO Box 708
Adams Basin, NY 14410-0708
Visit us at www.thewildrosepress.com

Publishing History
First Edition, 2021
Trade Paperback ISBN 978-1-5092-3783-8
Digital ISBN 978-1-5092-3784-5

Published in the United States of America

"What are you going to do to him?" She screamed like a banshee.

"Well, I'm just going to do to him whatever it takes for you to open that safe?"

"*No!* I told you I can't open it. Wait! Do something to me, not him. He's just a kid."

"Do you think I don't know that? Why do you think I picked him? And if after I'm done with him, you still don't open that safe, I'm gonna take that pretty little girlie over there. Oh, what me and my boys can do to her! I might even let Deet join in." Primo gave Deet a sly glance. "Wouldn't you like that, Deet, ole boy?"

Nora couldn't let any of that happen, but she couldn't think straight. Her mind raced to come up with some alternative while she focused on Primo's words. "No! Wait! Maybe we can handle it some other way."

"Old woman, if you think these studs would rather climb on top of your wrinkled ass instead of that sweet little juicy plum, you got a few screws loose in that head of yours."

His idea was revolting and far from what Nora had in mind. She was disgusted to even think about that possibility. God forbid. If she could oblige them in that manner to keep these kids safe, she'd do it in a heartbeat. But no chance of that happening. Like the monster said, these virile men thought of her as repulsive as she thought of them.

Praise for June Summers

BEFORE WE FADE AWAY:
"…just when you thought you had figured out who had done the crime, a new character was introduced and then came the twist…"

~Frances Neville, 5 stars

"…the book is filled with one surprise after another…held my attention from page one. There are vivid descriptions of the murders and one secret after another revealed. I highly recommend this book…"

~Paranormal Romance Review Team, 5 stars

LET FREEDOM RING:
"…such an original creative plot that pulls the reader into believing an almost unbelievable story line…an engrossing, unpredictable and enjoyable story."

~Michael V, 4 stars

"…once you start reading it you don't want to put it down until you're finished…"

~Christy, 5 stars

"…Good read…couldn't wait to find out how the story unfolded…"

~Betty Jane Evans. 5 stars

Dedication

As always, to Wendy, the candle in my life snuffed out
way too soon.
To Charles Howard—for so many reasons.
And to Chuck and Brenda—just because.

Chapter One

Tuesday Night

Who ever thought a tired and decrepit sixty-six-year-old woman like Nora Mitchell would need to fight for not only her own life, but also the lives of two of her dear grandchildren? Although she didn't know it at the time, this fierce battle between life and death started the night after she buried her husband Dave.

Nora's grandchildren, Sonya and Collin Suarez, planned to spend the summer with her to help their grandmother cope with the death of her husband. Northeastern Ohio was rather warm that May with temperatures creeping into the middle eighties for several days of the month. The kids spent most of the first day either swimming in the pool or out in the Jon boat on Lake Tenawa, the lake next to the Mitchell property.

About eight in the evening Nora sat on the screened porch watching the kids swim. Collin got out of the pool, draped his towel around his wet shoulders, and joined her on the porch, sitting on the chair across from her. "Granny, I'm kind of hungry. Can we get something else to eat besides that stuff left over from the funeral? It's tasting pretty yucky."

Agreeing with him, she chuckled. Dried sandwiches and stale cookies didn't sound too appetizing to her either. "We don't have much in the fridge, son, but I can drive into Sebring and get carry-out. What would you like?"

He puckered his lips and tilted his head to the side. "How about Zep's pizza?"

No restaurants delivered food to Smith Township in her part of Mahoning County, and Zep's Pizza Shop was six or seven miles away in Sebring. She needed to get out of the house anyway, needed to focus on something other than what to do with the rest of her life now that Dave was gone.

Dripping wet, Sonya also exited the pool, grabbed her towel from the patio, and walked through the porch door, volunteering, "I'll order it. What do we want?" She grabbed her phone from beside the couch and pulled up the pizza shop online.

"I want their Garbage Pizza," answered Collin. "It's so good with all that stuff on it."

"Order their breaded chicken wings and a couple of garden salads too," Nora added.

Sonya began keying in the number of the pizza shop. Looking up from her phone, she asked, "Oh, can I order a two liter bottle of cola, too? There's only bottles of water in the fridge. I like pop with pizza. Is that okay, Granny?"

"That's fine for now. Your mom is coming Friday night, and she said she'd bring some groceries for us until I feel like going shopping and cooking again."

After Sonya finished ordering the food, Nora got her purse from the hall closet. As she walked out the door to the attached garage, she called back, "I should be back in about forty-five minutes. Lock the door after I leave." In the garage, she hesitated before entering her minivan, looking over at Dave's shiny Mercedes parked next to her van. Tears invaded her eyes as she lamented his loss. "He loved that car so much."

As she got into her vehicle and pulled out of the garage, rain began to fall, not heavy, but steady. "Good," she said out loud. "We can use the rain. My poor flowers are so thirsty. I've neglected them lately." She turned the windshield wipers to intermittent speed as soon as she was on the driveway.

Traffic was almost nonexistent on Smith Garner Road all the way to West Middletown Road, where very few vehicles were also present. Because of the oily, slippery surface of the streets, it took her an extra five minutes to get to Zep's Pizza. Plus, she was probably more cautious than most drivers. She was the first to admit her eyesight and reflexes weren't what they used to be. What could an old woman expect?

Zep's had the pick-up pizza order ready as soon as she arrived. She paid the clerk, gave him a five-dollar tip, and went back out to her minivan with the rain getting heavier. She tucked the hot food containers on the floor of the back seat and hurried into the driver's seat. After starting up the minivan, she turned the windshield wipers to high, and they still had a difficult time keeping the windows clear. In addition, the cold rain pelting on the warm windows fogged them up a bit. Shaking her head, she realized she'd be even later than expected getting home. Somewhat nervous, she grasped the steering wheel tightly and focused intently on the road, wishing she never agreed to make this trip.

As she drove through the downpour and in spite of it, her thoughts wandered over the events of the past week, reminiscing about her happy life gone forever.

The relentless rain and her tears blurred her vision, making it more difficult to see the road ahead. Deep in thought, even sobbing with watery eyes, she suddenly saw bright lights coming directly toward her vehicle. A deafening horn unexpectedly blared, bringing her back to reality. She must have drifted into the left lane!

She immediately straightened the minivan onto her side of the road just seconds before a huge truck would've crashed head-on into her. She inhaled and exhaled a deep breath while her heart rapidly pounded against her ribs.

"You'd better pay attention, woman." Maybe she didn't want to live but endangering the lives of others was no way to end her own life. It really wasn't a matter of not *wanting* to live. She simply didn't know *how* she would live anymore without Dave.

The rain soon became a drenching deluge. To make things worse, when she turned onto West Middletown Road, the driver of the car behind her clicked on his bright lights, and she was blinded by the glare in her rearview mirror. She tried unsuccessfully to maneuver her head away from the glare. Then she slowed down even more than her already slow speed, thinking the driver might want to pass her and get on his way.

Instead, he rode her back bumper so close it looked like the hood of his huge vehicle swallowed the trunk of the minivan. She even rolled down her window and stuck out her left arm, soaking both her sleeve and arm, while waving and giving him the signal to go around her. But he unremittingly remained glued to her vehicle's back end with his lights on high beam, creating reflections that made it so hard, she barely saw anything. She debated if she should pull off the road.

Holding firmly to the steering wheel, she swiftly glanced out the passenger window. Because of the rainstorm, she couldn't determine what was along the edge of the road. Maybe trees. Perhaps mailboxes. For all she could tell, a person might be walking on the shoulder in the torrential rain. After a slight hesitation, she decided against pulling over.

The car behind Nora drove so close to her minivan that it forced her to increase her speed, going far faster than the weather conditions warranted. She was concerned how this was all going to end. Would they bang into her backend? Would they run her completely off the road so she crashed into a tree or a telephone pole? Were they actually trying to harm her? What kind of a dreadful end awaited her?

Finally, she caught sight of a narrow road immediately on her right. She swiftly twisted the steering wheel hard to the right to enter the turnoff, sliding, swerving, and almost going off the pavement into a ditch.

The demon car followed so fast and so close, it apparently was unable to make the turn and continued speeding straight ahead on West Middletown Road.

Struggling to keep her minivan on the road, Nora fleetingly noticed an abandoned building directly on her right. She raced into the vacant parking lot, immediately drove around to the back of the building, and shut off the car lights. She kept the car motor idling while she breathed heavily in and out, trying to calm her fractured nerves and slow her racing heartbeat.

What was happening? Why would some maniac target her?

After gaining some control over her emotions and

her heart rate, she coasted her minivan forward just enough to see the road from which she turned. She waited patiently in the dark, stormy night. Still, her breathing was heavy in the quiet of the silent car as she wondered if her nemesis would come back to taunt her again.

Nora didn't need to wait long. Within seconds, a large, dark vehicle—a truck, a van, or an SUV—passed the abandoned building at an alarming rate of speed. She was fairly certain it was the same intimidating vehicle that had ridden her tail for a couple of miles. It would probably be turning around soon when the driver realized her vehicle was no longer on the road ahead.

Within seconds, after the other vehicle passed the building, Nora put her car into reverse, screeched out of the parking lot onto the side road, and hurried back the way she came to West Middletown Road. She turned right at the stop sign and drove homeward as fast and as carefully as possible, concentrating only on driving and occasionally checking to see if the other vehicle had caught up to her. No more crying or searching memories.

She reached the turnoff onto Smith Garner Road without any other incidents, but her entire body still trembled like an agitator in a washing machine. At her property, she pulled onto the driveway, pressed the garage door opener, and coasted into the garage, still clutching the steering wheel with white knuckles and excessive force, almost releasing the garage door onto the trunk of the minivan.

When she stopped her vehicle and turned off the key, she threw her head back on the headrest and breathed deeply for a few seconds. *Why in hell was that vehicle targeting me?* Slowly, her mind came up with a few scenarios. Perhaps it was simply somebody in a hurry to get to a late appointment. But that didn't seem feasible, considering their threatening driving skills. It could have been a bunch of kids playing a sick, dangerous game with her life. Who knew what they had in mind if they caught up with her? She was so thankful to be safe at home. Maybe she wasn't ready to give up her life after all.

She sat in the car for a few more minutes, taking deep breaths and trying to compose herself before going into the house. She didn't want the kids to see how upset and shaken she was. As she sat regulating her breathing, Collin opened the door into the house. "Granny? Are you okay?"

Nora briskly bent toward the floor. "I'm fine. I just dropped my keys, but I've found them now. I'll be right in." She straightened her body and got out of the minivan.

Collin came into the garage and helped his grandmother carry the food into the kitchen. When they entered, Sonya was already setting out paper plates and napkins left over from the funeral. The three of them settled around the kitchen table eating their food. Nora's three dogs—Gordy, Cleo, and Amos—gathered at their feet, waiting to partake of anything that might drop on the floor. The three humans in the kitchen sometimes dropped a piece of pizza or a morsel of chicken to each of the dogs on purpose. They were happy and content to share in the delicious cuisine.

Nora's nerves calmed, and to her surprise, she felt decidedly hungry after the driving nightmare. Of course, she didn't mention it to the kids. No need to upset them any more than they were already by Dave's death. After all, he was their grandfather. Neither of them ever attended a funeral before. And to think the first one had to be someone they loved so dearly.

When they finished dinner, Sonya began organizing the leftovers, putting them in plastic containers or wrapping them in cling wrap. "Collin, help me put this stuff away."

Collin munched a final bite of his pizza and swallowed a deep gulp of his pop. He stood and gathered the throwaway containers. "That Garbage pizza was really good, Granny. Thank you. It's probably my favorite pizza ever. I wish there was a Zep's near our apartment."

"You're welcome, son. I enjoyed it, too." She became a bit melancholy, thinking about the many times she and Dave sat on the porch, eating Zep's pizza.

Nora ambled into the family room and turned on the television to watch the nightly news. After Sonya and Collin cleared away the leftovers and stored them in the fridge, they joined her for a while, occupying themselves on their smartphones while Nora tried to concentrate on the news, still emotionally drained from that horrid ride back from Zep's.

About a half hour later, Sonya arose from her chair, raised her arms, stretching her lithe body and yawning. "Granny, I'm gonna take my shower and go to bed. See you in the morning." She approached Nora and gave her grandmother a hug and a soft kiss on the cheek.

Nora lightly touched Sonya's arm. "Good night, dear. Thanks for staying with me."

With her phone in her hand, Sonya walked toward the hallway. "No problem. I'm enjoying it. Like Mom said, it gets boring at the apartment after a couple of weeks of summer vacation. There's so much more to do here." She turned and marched toward the stairs.

Collin was still playing a game on his phone. About ten minutes later, he raised his head and looked around the room as if he had forgotten where he was. Then he placed his phone on his lap. "Maybe I should get to bed, too. I'm kinda tired after fishing and boating all day." Closing out of his game, he slipped his phone into his back pocket. "Besides, I need energy to row the Jon boat tomorrow." He walked over to give Nora a hug. "Good night, Granny. See you in the morning."

"Good night, Collin. You do look a little tired."

After Collin went to bed, Nora was left alone with her three dogs and the murmur of the television in the background.

She began thinking about how things would be with the kids staying for the entire summer. They were helping her cope with Dave's loss, and to some degree keeping her mind off her untimely widowhood. Today, they fished from the Jon boat on Lake Tenawa. Sonya and Collin took turns rowing. The three of them also took a long walk in the woods, checking out and admiring all the late spring flowers and the growing summer foliage. The kids played in the forts Dave had built years ago for Brian and Amy, their adult children, while she continued walking the dogs near the lake. The grandkids seemed to be enjoying themselves, but they had just begun their summer break. They more than likely would become bored by the time August arrived and they would be returning to school.

After the kids were in bed and the house was quiet, Nora rehashed the earlier incident on her trip back from

Sebring. Thankfully, whoever it had been never caught up to her, but nonetheless, the whole ordeal was a frightening experience for an old lady.

At eleven o'clock, she got off the couch, turned off the television, and gathered up the dogs for their nightly potty break. Gordy yapped and jumped on her legs. Nora reached down and scratched his ears. "Good boy, good boy. Let's go outside."

The three dogs rushed through the screened porch to the outer doggie door with Cleo almost running over Gordy as she tried to be the first into the fenced yard. Nora smiled while she watched the dogs' antics— bounding onto the grass, smelling the ground, and taking care of their outside business while roaming and investigating the yard. They'd be her mainstay after the children went home.

Yes, the dogs would miss Dave too, especially Cleo. She was his dog, following him wherever he went on the property. It was like she was attached to his leg. But Dave didn't mind. He never needed to leash her. He loved that dog so much. At night she'd sleep on the rug on Dave's side of the bed. Amos would sleep on the one on Nora's side. Gordy thought he should sleep *on* the bed with Dave and her. Dave didn't mind him there either. The Mitchells had a California king-size bed, plenty of room for all three dogs, which wasn't such a good idea, considering the mass of Cleo and Amos' bodies. The two big ones also moved around too much. She and Dave would never be able to stay asleep.

The property on the back and sides of the house was huge with only a portion of it fenced in for the dogs' yard and the swimming pool. Beyond the fenced area, Dave had built a dock and a gazebo on Lake

Tenawa, where the two of them spent many evenings drinking cold beers, snacking on chips while watching the lake swallow the sun and waiting for the stars to break through the cobalt sky. The dogs would join them. Amos loved the water. He'd jump off the dock, swim around, attempting unsuccessfully to catch a fish, and then come back on the dock. He'd shake his long, black, silky hair of the access water before rejoining the couple in the gazebo. Nora would miss those nights so much. Perhaps she could still sit out there with the dogs, but it won't be the same.

While watching the dogs romp in the backyard, Nora turned on the outdoor lights and sat on the screened porch's white wicker couch. When the dogs tired of roaming, they joined her on the porch. Gordy jumped up beside her, circling at least ten times to get comfortable before he flopped down. Amos lay at her feet. In vain, Cleo searched the house for Dave before reluctantly joining the others again and jumping onto the matching wicker chair. She scratched the cushion until it was to her liking. Nora got off the couch momentarily to flick off the outdoor lights. The dogs remained resting after their nightly jaunt in the yard.

The rain expressed itself like thousands of fingers lightly tapping on the porch roof, now a steady, melodic sound, no longer that heavy inundation as earlier when she drove home from Sebring. Through the screening, she stared into the murky darkness, seeing nothing as Gordy lightly snored beside her. To add to the atmosphere, she decided to click on the CD of the music played at Dave's funeral, which consisted of his favorite songs from the sixties and seventies. She closed her eyes and rested her head on the soft couch cushion behind her while the harmonious melodies transported her back in time. Dancing with Dave at college events. Standing beside him at the church altar when they married. She and Dave enjoying their wedding day with friends and families. So many memories…

She must have dozed off, for she awakened when her cellphone rang. She searched for it in her pocket. "Hello, Amy."

"Mom, how did things go today with you and the kids?"

She didn't want to mention the issue with that disturbing vehicle. "Things went fine. The kids don't seem to be bored yet. They swam in the pool and played on the lake for most of the day."

Amy was silent for a couple of seconds. *"Mom? Uh, are you sure you're okay? This is a lot for you to handle at this time."*

"I'm okay—and the kids and I are doing just fine."

"I'll be out there Friday night. Is there anything special you want me to get at the grocery store?"

"Oh, you'd better ask Sonya and Collin what they want. I drove into Sebring and got Zep's pizza and chicken tonight. I'm not in much of a mood to cook."

"I'll cook this weekend. Tomorrow I'll ask them what they'd like me to buy." Again, Amy paused for a moment. *"Mom?"*

"What is it, dear?"

"You know I love you."

"I love you too. Don't worry about us. We'll be okay. See you Friday night."

Nora decided it was time to attempt sleep. She turned off the CD, got off the couch, and walked into the kitchen with the dogs following her. As she passed through the kitchen, she glanced at the wall clock over the sink. Ten minutes after midnight. She went upstairs to her bedroom, changed into her pajamas, pulled down the bedding, and climbed onto her side of the bed. However, she lay wide awake, tossing and turning, unable to sleep because her brain refused to give up thoughts about the traumatic experience earlier with the demon, black car.

When those frantic images eventually left her, then her mind started capturing incidents from the horrid previous week she had—Dave's heart attack, his death, his funeral. No way would she fall asleep with her mind so crowded with unhappy and disturbing thoughts and images.

She gave up. No use trying any longer. Getting out of bed, Nora went back downstairs into the kitchen and grabbed a glass of orange juice. She moseyed out to the screen porch with all three dogs close behind her. They probably couldn't sleep either. They missed Dave, too. They were so accustomed to him being around. How well she understood that!

A large portion of their property was covered with tall pines, oak and maple trees, dense foliage, and undergrowth—several simple acres of a plain, old Ohio woods. The kids always liked to play in those woods. Years ago, Dave built the first fort for Brian when he was about six. The two of them painted it a khaki green with black trim. It was a neat little structure raised off the ground about five feet. Dave built detachable steps to climb into the one room fort, which included cupboards, a table, and a few folding chairs, but leaving space for sleeping bags. It was great for Brian and his friends to play in and have sleepovers.

When Amy was about four, she claimed it was *her* playhouse. She and Brian fought so much over who was to play in it that Dave ended up building a second similar structure for Amy. She helped him paint it pink and purple. The building of this fort halted the fussing and arguing over whose turn it was to play in the original fort. And at last, the Mitchells had peace.

Dave kept the forts repaired even when Brian and Amy grew up and moved away. Thus, when Sonya and Collin came to visit, they also spent many hours playing in them. Now they can be used again by the grandkids for the entire summer.

Nora wasn't sure how long she sat on the porch, listening to the rain and reminiscing, regretting, and longing for what she no longer had. She glanced at her watch. To her surprise, it was after two o'clock. She should've gone back to bed, but she knew she wouldn't sleep. Just when she was about to get up and make another attempt at it, she spotted something in the woods off in the distance. It looked like a light shining around in the darkness, maybe near the boy's fort. Hard to tell. Remaining seated and concentrating where she thought she saw the flickering, she waited about ten more minutes, but the glimmer didn't appear again. She wouldn't be surprised if it was her mind playing tricks on her. With her lack of sleep lately, anything was possible.

While Dave lay so very ill in the hospital, Nora tried to sleep on a recliner near his bed. Then they put a cot next to him, but she didn't sleep then either. She felt she needed to spend every waking moment with him, knowing she had very few left. After his death and returning to their house, sleep still wouldn't come.

Since she apparently saw no more indications of any other light in the woods, she gathered her empty glass, put it in the dishwasher, locked the French doors to the porch, and climbed back up the stairs with Gordy, Amos, and Cleo following her.

Before attempting sleep again, she decided to take a hot shower. In the bathroom, she removed her pajamas and stepped into the shower. She turned the water on as hot as her body could stand it. She wanted to convince herself she was still alive, not a walking zombie. At the first jolt of the water on her skin, she wasn't sure if the water was ice cold or scalding hot. Either one created a similar instant reflex reaction. The water was hot. Very hot. She adjusted it so her wrinkled skin didn't begin peeling off in layers. But it did verify to her that she was definitely still alive. While lingering in the shower, she lifted her face to the spurting spray, closed her eyes, and allowed the water to have its medicinal effect. She wanted to remain there forever, not thinking, just feeling the hot, steamy mist on her weary body.

When she finally turned off the water and stepped out of the shower, her skin was not only wrinkled, but crinkled and red. With the house ghostly quiet, she towel dried her old body and dressed in her pajamas.

After relieving herself on the toilet, she walked down the hall to check on the kids. She quietly opened the door to Collin's room. He lay coverless in his boxers and a T-shirt in a fetal position smack in the middle of the double bed. Even though the boy had many of his dad's dark features, he was tall for his age, like Dave. At ten, he was already as tall as his sister. As he lay there, he looked so calm and relaxed. He should, after all the activity of the prior day.

Nora exited Collin's room, closing the door behind her. She strolled down the hall to Sonya's room. She lay on her back with her honey blonde hair billowing far out on the pillow top. She had the sheet tucked over her chest with her arms at her side. At fourteen, she was graceful, charming, and considerate—not always traits of young, teenage girls. Her mother needed to keep a close eye on her for the next few years. Like her mother, Sonya was destined to become a very pretty young lady.

Nora left Sonya's room and made her way back to her own bedroom, where she was positive she'd toss and turn the rest of the night. She settled on the bed once again—Gordy at her feet and the other dogs on their respective spots on the floor. Once she was situated, it was ghostly quiet. She heard only the sound of Gordy's soft snoring and the whirl of the ceiling fan above the bed. Every fifteen or twenty minutes, the air conditioner kicked on, discharging its frosty air into the room.

For what seemed like an eternity, she lay on the bed, staring at the ceiling, though it was far too dark to see anything even with the meager night light casting its narrow ray across the carpet. Maybe she should've done what Amy suggested earlier in the week and have Dr. Armstrong prescribe some type of sleeping aid. She hesitated taking any kind of medication that was not necessary for fear she might become dependent on them. But maybe she should.

Once again, she turned over in the bed. The sheets rustled from her movement, but did she also hear a different sound? Maybe one of the kids got up for a drink or to use the bathroom. She kept her body very still, holding her breath. She heard the sound again— like a dull cracking or tearing noise. It wasn't the kids. She knew they were sound asleep.

She sat upright in bed, tense and alert. She heard the sound again, even louder. Gordy's ears perked up. He must've heard it too. Cleo and Amos also sat up. Although it was too dark to see, Nora knew the hair on their backs stood straight up.

Someone was trying to break into the house.

Chapter Two

Early Wednesday Morning

Dave always kept a twelve-inch iron pipe underneath their bed. For the most part, he was a nonviolent man. However, he often told her, "I'll do anything necessary to keep you and the kids safe, even if it meant going against my beliefs."

When Nora heard those strange noises a third time, she was alert and wide awake. She quickly draped on her robe, stepped into her slippers, and seized the iron pipe from under the bed. Without hesitating, she scampered down the stairs as softly as possible with the pipe, upright and ready, gripped tightly in her hand. All three dogs jumped up and scurried after her.

In the kitchen, she turned on the ceiling light, its brightness temporarily blinding her. The French doors to the screen porch were still locked securely just as she left them earlier. From inside the kitchen, she flicked on the screened porch light and unlocked the doors. Looking around, she saw nothing out of place—until her eyes focused on the doggie door. The frame was severely mangled and broken. Hmm...

Nora retrieved her high-powered flashlight from the drawer of the end table next to the wicker couch. She turned on the outdoor lights that illuminated the pool area as well as the landscaped part of the yard.

Only the dense foliage of the wooded part of the property lay in total darkness.

When she opened the door to go outside, her flashlight reflected on several sharp pieces of the doggie door's frame lying on the porch carpet and the concrete patio. The dogs followed her through the doorway, sniffing frantically around the patio pavement and sensing something unusual. She stepped to the edge of the patio and scanned the area but saw nothing out of the ordinary. She moved off the patio and walked around the pool but found no evidence of anything unusual. Shining the flashlight behind the utility shed where the power lights didn't reach, she determined nothing unfamiliar or concerning lurked there either. Coming around the front of the shed, she examined the shed door. It was still securely locked.

Nora returned to the porch and put away the flashlight. She stared at the broken doggie door. Probably some large raccoon or possum tried to get to the dish of dog food left on the porch. Maybe even a fox, a wolf, or a coyote. She often heard the cries of a pack of coyotes late at night coming from the woods, their poignant howls piercing the darkness with her dogs sometimes joining in the choral arrangement. This was not the first time that critters tried to invade the screened porch. Although, they were usually not large enough to damage the doggie door so badly.

Maybe a false alarm. She'd have to put in a new doggie door. Looked like she needed to make a trip to Leonard's Hardware Store in Sebring soon. She didn't want the dogs cutting themselves on the sharp plastic left behind on the frame. Until she was able to get to Leonard's, she needed to give it a temporary fix. From the utility room, she took a broom, a dustpan, and a large plastic bag and cleaned up the broken pieces off the porch and the patio. When she returned to the utility room to put away the supplies, she noticed she had several rolls of duct tape. Determining that the tape could provide a temporary fix, she grabbed one roll. Back on the porch, she mended the jagged edges of the doggie door.

After cleaning up the mess, she went back into the kitchen, locked the French doors, turned off all the lights, and trotted back upstairs. The dogs followed close behind. She replaced the iron pipe under the bed and removed her robe and slippers before crawling into bed once again for another attempt at sleep. Gordy climbed up his doggie stairs and scurried round and round at Nora's feet until he was comfortable. And Amos and Cleo settled in their spots on the floor.

Nora spent the remainder of her night tossing and turning. Maybe someday she'd be able to sleep again like a normal person. Countless times she inadvertently stretched her arm to the other side of the bed only to touch the cold, crisp surface of the empty sheet next to her. She could not get used to that vacant space. She could not get used to being without Dave. The funeral was the last time she was able to look at her dear husband's face. She never wanted to forget it. Already the image was growing dim.

Chapter Three

The Previous Monday (The Day of the Funeral)

Nothing was right. The weather was supposed to be drizzly with dark, threatening clouds and blustery breezes blowing through the barren trees. Anyhow, that was how it was portrayed in the movies. The spring's cheerful sun shouldn't burst through the windows like a fire storm with Nora sitting in her living room on the overstuffed couch surrounded by so many people, some she didn't even recognize.

The air conditioner shouldn't spurt cool, dry air from its vents, keeping those strangers comfortable while she was drowning in utter despair, wishing everyone would go away. How could they chat softly and smile as they consumed the sandwiches, the salads, and the cookies from the buffet on the dining room table? Or sip their coffee while they checked out who else was in the room. Or look at their smartphones, wondering when to leave discreetly. They meant well, at least most of them. They felt sorry for her, and they came to support her, to show they cared, or to show their respect. But she just wanted to be left alone with her grief and her sorrow. She couldn't take all their condolences and sympathy. She wished they'd all leave, every one of them.

Amy sat down on the couch beside Nora. "Mom,

do you want a sandwich or something to drink? How about a cup of tea?"

"No, dear, I'm fine." She felt like screaming and kicking every person out of the house.

"No, you're not fine. You just buried Dad. How can you say you're fine?"

Amy was right. Nora wasn't fine at all. How could she be? Forty-one years. Almost forty-one years she and Dave were married. So how could she be fine when the man she loved, the man she spent most of her life with, the father of her children, was snatched from her. Poof! Gone.

She would never see his smile again. She would never hear his laughter, the deep, gruff tone always making her laugh with him no matter her mood. She'd never lie beside him again and feel the warmth of his strong body, his living body snuggled next to hers. It hurt. It hurt more than any pain she ever felt in her entire life. More than any physical pain—childbirth included. More than any financial distress—like living on dollar store noodle soup during her college years. More than any other loss—even her parents' sudden deaths. It hurt to her very soul. And she couldn't make the pain go away. No one could.

Amy gently touched her arm. "You have to eat something, Mom. When was the last time you ate anything?"

Nora stared out the living room picture window. She glanced at the glistening rays of sun as the streaks of light bounced off the metal butterfly sculpture sticking up in her yard's spring flower garden. She hadn't tended to the flowers lately. Since it hadn't rained in days, they needed watering. Poor things. They were so deceivingly bright and beautiful, so opposite from her emotions. The white lilies-of-the-valley with their bell flowers clinging close to the ground engulfed by the vivid purple and yellow pansies. The tall irises with the silky, pastel petals sprouting downward. Peonies with their rich pinks and cheerful whites.

"Mom?" Amy prodded.

"What... What did you say, dear?"

"You need to eat something."

The butterflies on the sculpture danced in the sunlight, flapping their thin, vibrant wings in the gentle breeze. Perhaps they might break loose from their base and fly away. Just like Dave. Fly out of Nora's life. Just like her Dave.

"Mom!" Amy's voice seemed urgent.

Nora turned to face her. She heard herself speak in a hollow voice, "What is it, dear?"

Amy got off the couch. "I'm getting you a sandwich. You haven't eaten for days. You need to get something in your stomach."

Nora watched Amy walk toward the dining room to get her something to eat from the buffet. Then Nora looked out the window again. In the yard, a red cardinal perched stoically on a limb of the maple tree. Don't they say a cardinal is the sign of a message from a spirit? *Oh, Dave. I don't want your spirit; I want you in the flesh. Why did you leave me? How can I go on without you?*

Amy returned and placed a sandwich on a paper plate on the end table beside Nora. "Mom, please. Eat the sandwich." Amy's eyes stared dolefully as she tried to convince her mother to eat. "Please."

Nora picked up the sandwich, gazed at it as if it

were a foreign object she never saw before, and took a small bite. She wrinkled her nose and frowned. It tasted like cardboard. She had difficulty chewing and swallowing even the smallest of morsels. Her mouth felt dry and grainy. With a scowl, she placed the sandwich back on the plate.

"Good. That's a start," praised Amy. Her mournful smile touched Nora's heart. She knew her daughter was grieving too. Amy deeply loved her dad and would truly miss him.

Nora continued looking out the front window. A drab brown female cardinal joined the fiery red male. They say cardinals mate for life. Just like her and Dave. For life. But Dave's life ended. Not Nora's. What would she do with the rest of hers without him? She wondered what the cardinal would do if his mate was killed by a cat or a hawk. Would he find another mate to take her place? *Keep her close, pretty red bird. Don't let her out of your sight. You can't live without her.*

Once again, Nora reached for the sandwich and tried another bite. It still tasted like cardboard. Amy noticed her mother frown as Nora replaced the sandwich back on its plate. "Let me get you some water. The sandwiches are a little dry."

Nora's eyes followed Amy as she walked to the dining room. Amy selected a bottle of water from the credenza and walked toward Nora while struggling to open the miniscule cap from the flimsy plastic bottle.

Dressed in her modest black skirt and lacey, gray blouse—quite unusual for her—Sonya sat on one of the side chairs. When she saw her mother having difficulty with the cap, Sonya went to help Amy open the water bottle. Nora watched the two of them. Sonya looked bored. Nora knew her granddaughter didn't want to be at this house for this occasion. She'd rather be with her friends. Teenagers don't understand death. That's probably a good thing. But Nora knew Sonya missed her grandfather too and wouldn't want to be anywhere but by her grandmother's side to support her.

Amy smiled at her daughter as Sonya took the bottle from her, gripped it gently, opened the cap with ease, and handed it back to her mother. Amy accepted the bottle and mouthed a soft "thank you" to Sonya.

They looked so much alike, Amy and Sonya. Like Dave too. Not masculine, though. Their faces converted his rugged, male features into soft, delicate, feminine ones. His curly, blond hair so often hard to tame; Amy's a creamy blonde while Sonya's more a honey blonde. Amy's eyes were blue, like Dave's. Sonya's were an iridescent blue-green, shimmering and changing color with whatever she wore.

Amy sat back down beside Nora and handed her the water bottle while Sonya returned to her chair and stared into space. Nora lifted the bottle to her lips and drank a sip. It was lukewarm, but it helped wash down the cardboard sandwich bites.

As they silently sat on the couch, Amy and Nora both stared out the window. A couple of boys had gathered near the maple tree. Nora's grandson Collin awkwardly stood there in his new, dark suit. Benny and Dalton, his friends, stood next to him. They, in contrast, wore shorts and T-shirts.

Collin looked more like his father—not Amy. Not Dave either. Sable brown hair, dusky eyes, and coppery skin. Nora was glad Collin's friends stopped by. The boys were talking, but Collin seemed to be distracted, kicking at a stick beneath the maple tree. Poor Collin. He admired Dave so much.

Collin and his friends walked away from Nora's view. She then turned her vision away from the window. In the distance, she heard Gordy yapping and whimpering. He was a sweetheart, but his bark could be annoying. Before people gathered at the house, Collin had closed the three dogs in the utility room to keep them from getting underfoot as the guests moved about. Amos and Cleo were quiet. They raised a raucous only when they felt annoyed or threatened. But Gordy, he had always been a yapper.

Then Nora's eyes wandered around, looking at the faces of those gathered in her house. Her son Brian was smiling and talking to a few other men standing next to him near the dining room table covered with food. He nonchalantly reached for one of the decorative cookies near him. As he bit into the cookie, he nodded his head, responding to something he agreed with that one of the other men had said.

Brian looked more like Nora but tall like his dad. Although sprinkles of gray were beginning to invade his closely cropped, chocolate brown hair, he was still a handsome man. Sometimes he could be an arrogant asshole. Nora felt she could say that because she was his mother. Where his personality came from was beyond her.

Maybe his snobbish wife Lisa had something to do with it, although Nora had doubts about that. He had always thought himself superior to others. He had done well for himself. She had to agree, and she was proud of him. Both he and Lisa were corporate attorneys and partners in the prestigious Cleveland law firm of

Mitchell, Mitchell, Willis, and Drake. But Nora thought their success had gone to their heads.

Looking quite animated, her other grandson, Marcus, stood next to Brian. Nodding his head, Marcus was engaged in whatever his dad and the men were discussing. He was a freshman at Brian's alma mater, Ohio State University in Columbus, studying to be an attorney. She hoped he didn't turn out like his father and mother. So far, he was a good kid. Intelligent too.

Dave was proud of all his family. Nora used to argue with him about Brian, but he'd tell her, "Someday, dear, he'll show you he's not such a bad guy. You'll see." That hadn't happened yet, and the man was almost forty. She wasn't sure when that change would come.

In spite of his rotten personality, Nora dearly loved Brian. He was her son. How could she *not* love him? But sometimes she didn't like him. Was that an awful thing for a mother to say? Probably.

As for Amy, she was a darling. She'd do just about anything for anybody. She donated to official charities and individuals in need even when her funds were not that plentiful. Her friends knew who to call on when they needed a favor, large or small. Look how she tried to care for her mother. It wasn't Amy's fault she didn't cooperate.

Also near the table sipping a bottle of water was Carlos Suarez, Amy's ex-husband. At the gravesite, he had sat directly behind Amy and the kids with his hand on Amy's shoulder. Standing there in the dining room, he looked uncomfortable in his charcoal gray suit, all alone. He probably wanted to be anywhere but there. It was nice of him to stop by. Even though his marriage to

Amy ended, Nora still felt he was part of the family. Sonya stood with him earlier. She had rested her head against him while he placed his arm around her. Nora had observed her granddaughter smiling meekly as he spoke. Nora was glad he was there to comfort Sonya. Their parents may be estranged, but Collin and Sonya still loved them both.

Finally, the people in the house began to leave. One by one they approached Nora. "So sorry, Nora; our prayers are with you, dear; Nora, keep strong; Nora, if there's anything I can do..." and on and on. In response, she nodded her head to each of them, "Thank you, thank you, thank you"—over and over again until all who remained were family and the caterers, who began clearing away the buffet.

In the yard, the cardinals were gone from the maple tree, but the metal butterflies still precariously clung to their base, still gently flapping their colorful, shimmery wings.

The family all gathered in the living room. Brian sat next to Nora, placing his hand on her knee. He tilted his head toward her. "Mom, why don't you come stay with Lisa and me for a few weeks. There's nothing to keep you here now."

Nora's icy eyes glared at him. "I know that, Brian. Your dad is dead."

Brian shook his head defensively. "I didn't mean it like that. It just that, well, what will you do with yourself now that Dad is gone?"

"What would I do with myself at your place? You and Lisa will be at work. Marcus goes back to the university. Should I keep your cleaning lady company? Or maybe you can fire her; I could do her job. With that big house of yours, I'd definitely keep busy."

She didn't know why she said those things to Brian. Maybe everything was just catching up to her. But she had to admit—she *did* know who Brian took after. Dave always told her to think before she spoke. She had a difficult time learning that courtesy.

"Come on, Mom. Don't be so sarcastic. There's plenty of things to do around Cleveland that you've never seen or done before. You like the beach. There's several of them nearby. We have a few escape rooms that are fun. The amusement park isn't too far away. You always liked roller coasters, and they have the best in the country. There's also a couple of playhouses and musical venues close by. We even have a few comedy clubs you could attend. You can spend as much time as you wish with us. Lisa can show you the best places to shop. You won't be bored."

She knew Brian was simply trying to be helpful. She realized she could be a bitch at times. Sometimes she and Brian would butt heads. If she was honest with herself, she had to admit it wasn't always his fault.

She clasped her son's hand. "I'm so sorry, Brian. You're right. That was unkind and unfair and very rude. Forgive me." She squeezed his hand as she lightly shook her head. "But I'll feel more comfortable here for now." She released his hand and patted his thigh. "Maybe in a couple of months I'll come stay with you, but not now."

Did Nora see Lisa breathe a sigh of relief?

Brian gently clutched his mother's hand with both of his and kissed her on the cheek. "Okay, Mom. I understand." He got off the couch. "We're going to start back to Hunting Valley. Marcus has to leave for campus tomorrow morning. I'll give you a call this weekend. But if you change your mind or if you need anything, please call me. Okay?"

"I will, dear. I'm really sorry for what I said. Please forgive me."

"Already done, Mom."

Lisa and Marcus gave Nora hugs before they left with Brian and drove away in their shiny, new Porsche.

Amy and Sonya took Brian's place next to Nora on the couch. Amy glanced at the dry sandwich on the end table. "You didn't eat any more of the sandwich. Do you want something else?"

With a grimace on her face, Nora also looked at the sandwich. "No. I'm not hungry."

Sonya leaned across her mother's lap to look toward her grandmother. She had a twinkle in her eyes. "Granny, how about some ice cream? I saw some strawberry in the freezer. That's your favorite. How about if I get both of us some?"

Sonya, like her mother, always thought of others.

"Sure, honey, I'd like that." She really wasn't in the mood for ice cream either, but the girl wanted to help. The least she could do was to accept her offer.

Collin, sitting on the chair across from the females, had removed his jacket and tie and draped them over the back of the chair. He looked a bit more comfortable. "Sonya, I'll take some too, please. Chocolate for me if Granny has it."

"I'll check." Sonya arose from the couch and walked toward the kitchen.

Amy tilted her head, smiling cheerily. "Well, I guess ice cream is better than nothing."

Nora gave her a small grin. "Better than dried, stale

sandwiches that taste like cardboard."

Before Sonya returned with the ice cream, Amy clasped her mother's hand. "Mom, Brian is right. I don't want you to be alone out here either. You're too isolated. I've talked to the kids. They've finished all their final exams for the year. They don't really need to go to school these last few days. We think it's best if they stay out here with you for a while. Perhaps for the entire summer. There's lots for them to do here with the pool, the lake, and the surrounding woods. Of course, they have their phones to keep in touch with their friends. Besides, two of Collin's friends were out front with him today. One of their mothers dropped them off to pay their respects to him. So maybe they could come out some other time too. Maybe after you get used to Sonya and Collin being around."

"Oh, I don't know, dear. They won't want to spend much time here. They'd be bored."

"Mom, I talked about it with them. They're okay with it. I'd stay myself, but I have to be at the office by six in the morning until six every night. My vacation is in July. I could come join the three of you then. And I'll be here on weekends too."

Nora rubbed her hand over her forehead and shook her head. "I don't know."

"What don't you know, Granny?" Sonya asked as she brought the bowl of strawberry ice cream to Nora.

"Oh, your mother has some cockamamie idea about you and Collin staying here with me for all or part of the summer. I doubt if that's a good idea."

Sonya handed Nora her dish of strawberry ice cream and then walked over to Collin, giving him his chocolate. She sat on the opposite chair to eat hers.

"Why not? I think it'd be fun. Remember when we used to stay here when we were younger? You and I would always make things. Remember those earrings we made Mom from that kit you bought? She still wears them. Don't you, Mom?"

Amy smiled and bobbed her head. "Yes, I do. I always liked them."

Sonya was doing her best to convince her grandmother. "And Gramps and Collin used to go fishing in the lake. Gramps would take us all out in the Jon boat. We'd have so much fun rowing across the lake. He'd let us do the rowing. We both got pretty good at it, didn't we Collin?"

Collin was licking the chocolate from his mouth. "Yeah, Gramps and I used to catch lots of fish. All kinds of them. But we usually threw them back into the lake." He dipped his spoon into his ice cream again.

After taking a bite of her ice cream, Nora turned toward Sonya. "Your grandpa isn't here to go fishing or boating anymore."

"But we can still do it. The three of us. Right? It'd be fun."

Collin shoveled another spoonful of chocolate ice cream into his mouth and licked his lips again. "Granny, I'm ten now, you know. I can take care of the boat. Gramps showed me. I'm good at fishing too. I can show you if you don't know how."

Nora stared at her hands holding the ice cream bowl. Then she looked up at Amy, whose eyes pleaded with her. "See, Mom. They want to stay. It'll be good for them *and* you. They'd be bored at the apartment all summer. They tell me this every summer about two weeks after school ends. There's so much to do out

32

here, and the three of you can do it together. What do you say?"

Nora did think it might be nice to have the kids around. It'd been ages since they stayed for more than a day. Even then, Amy usually stayed too. Nora couldn't remember the last time the kids stayed overnight. Like Amy insisted, maybe it'd be good for her. They won't help her forget about the pain of losing Dave, but they would lessen it a little. At least for a while. She looked from Sonya to Collin. "Are you kids sure you want to stay here?"

Between mouthfuls of ice cream, both of them shouted, "Yes!"

Amy and the kids left to pack their clothes and whatever else they planned to bring to Nora's house. The caterers cleaned up what remained of the food and the mess. Then they also left. Nora was alone again in a house that seemed deadly silent. She stared out the window for a while longer, thinking the red cardinal might return, but he didn't.

Finally, she forced herself off the couch and released the dogs from the utility room for a much needed potty break in the back yard.

Before the kids returned, she freshened up the bedrooms for them. There wasn't much to really do. The bedding was already clean, but she hadn't dusted or vacuumed for some time, with Dave getting sick and all. So she polished the furniture and ran the vacuum. It gave her something constructive to do and helped take her mind off her misery.

A few hours later, Amy and the kids returned with their things and carry-out for dinner. They sat at the kitchen table. Nora actually ate a few fries and about a half of her cheeseburger.

Amy left after dinner. "I'll be back Friday night after work. If you need anything, give me a call."

"I will, dear. See you Friday night, then."

The kids cleared away the carry-out trash and went to their respective rooms. They got on their phones, texting, playing games, or whatever else kids do with those things. They were on vacation. Nora wanted them to feel comfortable and enjoy their time here. She would try her best to make that work.

Chapter Four

Dave's funeral was Monday. The kids slept late on Tuesday morning and hung out at the pool with the dogs for most of the afternoon. They snacked on leftovers all day until that evening when Nora went for pizza and had that terrible car experience. Then, after an almost sleepless night riddled with strange noises, mysterious lights, and raw emotions, she was in the kitchen Wednesday morning at eight o'clock, hopefully ready for a better day.

"How about pancakes this morning, kids?" she asked as Sonya and Collin walked into the kitchen while rubbing the sleep out of their eyes. At least Nora was starting to do things besides sitting and staring out the window, watching birds, flowers, and fake butterflies.

Collin's eyes lit up. "Oh, boy! We haven't had pancakes for breakfast in *forever*. Mom never has the time to fix them. All we get is cereal or toast."

Sonya gave Collin a disdainful look. "That's not true, Collin. Sometimes Mom fixes us big breakfasts on weekends. Sometimes she makes us bacon and eggs, too. You just have to ask her. That's all." Then Sonya asked Nora, "Granny, do you have any strawberry jam? I like that on my pancakes now."

35

Nora opened the fridge and looked on the door shelves. "Yes, I do. I might try that; it sounds tasty."

Collin sat down at the table. "How about Nutella? Do you have any of that?"

Nora shook her head. "I'm afraid not. I haven't bought that in ages. I'll ask your mom to get it for us when she goes to the grocery store."

"That's okay. I'll just have syrup then. Do you have that?"

"Oh yes, I have maple or blueberry syrup."

Nora took out the ingredients to make the pancakes. Sonya set the table while Collin got them milk to drink. Nora was already on her second cup of coffee, sipping it as she prepared the pancakes.

As they ate breakfast, Sonya asked, "Granny, do you think it'd be okay if we invited some friends over today? Kyle, my one friend, said his mom will drive them out here. I know Mom said maybe next week, but I can text her and tell her if it's okay with you."

Collin had just taken a gulp of milk. "Oh, boy! That'd be fun. Can I invite Benny and Dalton? We can play in the forts and swim in the pool. Maybe we could go out on the Jon boat, too."

Nora put her fork down while she contemplated their idea. "I guess it'd be okay. You'll have to tell your mother about it just in case she strongly disagrees for some reason."

"I'll text her before I let Kyle know you said yes."

Nora took a bite of her pancakes, then countered Collin's plan. "But no Jon boat on the lake. I know, Collin, you and your sister can handle the boat, but I don't feel up to being responsible for all of your friends, too. Maybe you can have them back later in the summer when I'm more up to going out on the boat with you."

After breakfast, Sonya called their mom. Amy thought it was unwise so soon after Dave's death, but Nora told her it'd be good for the children. Definitely having a bunch of kids around would keep Nora busy and keep her mind somewhat off her loneliness and despair.

Sonya and Collin called their friends and arranged for them to come about eleven. Sonya suggested they fix hot dogs for lunch. Nora took the frozen hot dogs and buns out of the freezer so they'd be defrosted by lunchtime.

"Can we make some brownies too, Granny?" asked Sonya.

Nora squinted her eyes. "Let me check if I have a box of brownie mix." She looked in the cupboard. "Ah, here's a chunky brownie mix. Will that do?"

"Perfect!" declared Sonya.

They made the brownies once they cleared away the breakfast dishes. When they were out of the oven, they set the brownies on the kitchen counter to cool.

Sonya also suggested, "We could maybe eat the bags of chips and other snacks left over from the funeral for lunch, too."

"Great idea, dear. I didn't know how else I'll get rid of them."

Sonya's friends arrived shortly after eleven. As they stood outside, she introduced them to Nora. "Granny, these are my friends." She pointed to a pretty, caramel haired girl with big brown eyes, high cheekbones, and a smattering of freckles on her nose. She was dressed in cut-off jean shorts and a pink T-shirt with a photo on the front of somebody named Harry Styles. "This is Jenna. She's my best friend."

Sonya then waved her hand toward the tall, lanky boy with the black-framed glasses and short cropped, tawny brown hair. He too was dressed in cut-off jeans and an Austintown Fitch T-shirt. "That's Kyle, over there. He's the tall one."

The other kid was small in stature, looking about twelve or thirteen. He had bronzed skin, deep set, dark eyes, and ink-black, curly hair falling almost to his shoulders. He had on black shorts and a plain gray V-neck T-shirt. Sonya motioned toward him. "The one on the end is Deet."

Nora looked dubiously at this one who fidgeted and kept looking down at the ground. "Is that your real name, Deet?"

The boy looked up and answered, "No, ma'am. It's Diego. Deet's my nickname. My little sister couldn't pronounce Diego when she was small. So now everybody calls me Deet."

"How old are you?" Perhaps she was being a little nosy, but she was curious why he'd be hanging out with the other kids, who looked more like Sonya's age.

"I turned sixteen last week, ma'am."

"Oh! I'm sorry. I thought you were younger."

"That's okay. I get that all the time. I'm just small for my age. My mom is short, too."

Sonya started leading the kids out the back door. "Granny, we'll be in the girl's fort. Call us when lunch is ready, okay?"

Nora watched as they left the fenced property and entered the wooded area. Deet looked back and waved at her. With a puzzled look, she raised her arm and returned the wave.

About twenty minutes later, Collin's friends, who had been at the house the day of the funeral, also arrived. Collin introduced Nora to Dalton's mother before she drove away. Collin, Dalton, and Benny ran off toward the boy's fort. His grandmother yelled to them as they scurried away, "I'll call you when lunch is ready."

She planned to start lunch around one o'clock since she assumed the kids wouldn't be ready to eat for a while. They'd want to hang out in the forts. In the meantime, she and the dogs settled on the porch and watched as the boys disappeared into the trees on their way to their fort. When they were out of sight, her mind began to wander again back to her life with Dave.

Nora met Dave when they both attended Youngstown State University. She was starting her freshman year. He was a big-shot senior on campus, a star basketball player. In her wildest dreams, she never thought he'd ever notice her, a mere freshman. Well, actually, he didn't have much of a choice, since she bumped right into him, literally. Nora Jean Chambers considered herself a country hick from Craig Beach, Ohio, a small village on Lake Milton of about two thousand people. The town's claims-to-fame were its beach, fishing, boating, and the old local amusement park, now gone forever. Very exciting. Ho-hum.

David Charles Mitchell was a guy from the big city of Youngstown—at least back then Nora thought of it that way. Being her first week at the university, she was enthralled with the campus. It was so big, so unique from her limited life experiences. Craig Beach didn't even have its own high school. She was bussed to

Jackson-Milton High in North Jackson, which was a far cry from the campus at the university.

Their chance meeting happened while Nora was turning around, overloaded with new textbooks she had just purchased, scoping out the enormity of her surroundings, and wondering how she'd ever find her way around the myriad of buildings and pavements. Walking backward with her mesmerized eyes gazing everywhere but where they should have been, she suddenly hit a moving obstacle, David Mitchell. Her textbooks flew from her arms and tumbled to the ground, as also did her overloaded body. Before she even realized what had happened, she was being lifted to her feet. When she turned around, she found herself staring into an artist's cartoon rendition of a penguin on a red T-shirt. Slowly, she raised her head while focusing her eyes inch by inch along their journey. It felt like an eternity before they arrived at the face belonging to that Penguin shirt.

This guy had to be nine feet tall. Well, maybe not nine feet, more like six feet, five inches. As for Nora? She was lucky if she even reached the five-foot, one inch mark. He was a giant. Wisps of his curly, flaxen-blond hair lay across his ears. His sharp features were chiseled perfectly in his deeply tanned, lean face. And those eyes! She had never seen such a brilliant, cerulean blue. They drew her in immediately. She was in love. She couldn't speak. She simply stared at this Adonis.

"Uhh, are you okay?" A velvety, mellow voice took her out of her trance.

"I...I'm so sorry! I wasn't looking where I was going. So sorry," she stammered while trying to gracefully stoop to the pavement to recover her books.

This godly specimen of a man reached down to help her pick them up. "Yeah, I guess not." His deep voice flowed from his luscious mouth.

After the books were retrieved, he gently grabbed her arm and helped her stand again. "Oh, you're bleeding! Your elbow."

She twisted her arm around her books to see for herself. Sure enough, droplets of blood oozed from a nasty scrape on the side of her arm. So enthralled by this towering giant, she never felt any pain.

"You'd better get that taken care of. Are you on your way to class?" He was still holding onto her arm.

"Uh, no. I just got my books at the bookstore. Uh, I was going to my car." She was still somewhat tongue-tied in the presence of this hot guy.

He checked his watch. "I have a few minutes. Let me walk you to First Aid and get that injury seen to."

"That's okay. I'm fine. It's just a little scrape. I should've been more careful. I'm really sorry."

"It's more than a scrape. Come on. Give me your books. You're going to First Aid with me." He took all the books from her while handing her his handkerchief. "Here. Put this on the wound to stop the bleeding. Follow me."

So she did follow him.

It wasn't until they were waiting for the nurse in the First Aid office that they even introduced themselves. And that was it for Nora. She followed him for the rest of his life.

****

After Dave graduated from Youngstown State, he began his career as a civil engineer at the Akron Canton Airport in North Canton. Nora got her teaching degree a few years later and taught fifth grade at Parkway Elementary School in Alliance, Ohio. She and Dave were married the summer after her second year of teaching. They lived in an apartment in Alliance for a couple of years. After Brian was born, they built the house on Smith Garner Road in Smith Township, a few miles from Sebring. Amy was born six years after Brian's birth.

Their beautiful home sat on thirty acres of land. The four-bedroom colonial was located about two hundred yards from the road and about sixty yards from the lake. Nora obtained a teaching job at Damascus Elementary School, but when Brian started BL Miller Elementary in Sebring, that school had an opening for a fifth-grade teacher. She transferred from Damascus Elementary so she would have the same schedule as Brian. The family lived a comfortable life as their children grew, got their education, and moved on. Dave and Nora both retired two years ago, hoping to travel and enjoy things they never experienced before. That didn't last for very long. It ceased when Dave had his heart attack.

****

Nora was dozing and pondering about her happy life now gone when she was suddenly awakened by the screen door slamming shut. She quickly opened her eyes to see Collin and his two friends standing in the doorway. Out of breath, Collin blurted, "Granny, somebody's been in the fort."

His words brought her wide awake and alert. "What? How do you know that?"

"Because there's cigarette butts on the floor and beer cans on the table."

Her heart skipped a beat. She recalled the flash of light she'd seen in the early morning hours; the noise she'd heard; the broken doggie door. She got up from the couch, trying to sound nonchalant. "It's probably some poor, homeless person escaping the rain last night. Let me come and take a look."

She grabbed Amos and Cleo's leashes from the utility room. Collin helped her fasten them to the dogs' collars. With her holding onto Amos, Collin holding Cleo's leash, and Gordy trotting beside them, they plodded toward the woods.

Over the years, paths were worn leading to the forts, which were built about two hundred yards into the woods. Since those trails had not been used on a regular basis, they were somewhat thicker with foliage and small shrubs, but still discernable. The branches of forsythia bushes and butterfly weed dipped in front of them, requiring them to occasionally duck beneath the bushes or push them away. Hearty purple longstrife and cut-leaved teasel brushed their legs as they walked. The forts themselves were about fifty yards apart with the path splitting about a hundred seventy yards from the fenced part of the property.

The air was very still and heavy as they maneuvered the awkward path. They began to hear the laughter and chatter of Sonya and her friends the closer they got to the forts. When they came to the split in the path, Collin automatically led the group toward the boy's fort. At the site, Amos, Gordy, and Cleo frantically sniffed the ground. An intruder had certainly been there. And recently. Nora and Collin tied the dogs to the pillars supporting the fort, and with some effort, Nora climbed up the wooden staircase. Gordy continued sniffing on the ground around the perimeter.

The inside of the fort reeked of stale cigarettes and spilled beer. In places, the cigarette butts had actually charred the wooden floor, and sticky beer residue dazzled as the sun shone through the trees and window space onto the table in the middle of the small room. Nothing else was destroyed or disturbed. Whoever was here must've waited out the storm and then left. But why? What reason would anyone have to be walking around this area of the county? Only private property was in this vicinity. No businesses of any kind. So what was anybody doing here?

Nora's thoughts soon channeled in a different direction. Was this trespasser connected in any way to the broken doggie door? Her fleshy skin broke out in goosebumps, and her wrinkled forehead moistened with perspiration. However, she didn't want to show the kids her fear. "How about if you boys pick up the cans and the cigarettes. I'll go back for a garbage bag and a bucket of soapy water to clean off the table and floor. You can't play here the way this is."

The boys started their task as she struggled backward down the ladder and untied the two dogs from the posts. She marched with them back to the house. Were her fears unfounded? Probably. It just seemed strange that both the doggie door was mangled and Collin found evidence someone invaded the fort.

Nora stopped suddenly in the pathway, Gordy running into her. *What about that incident last night with the dark vehicle following me?* She began walking again. *Don't be absurd. These are just random occurrences. Don't make a mountain out of a molehill.*

In the utility room at the house, she gathered a

trash bag, a bucket, a scrub brush, and some rags. She filled the bucket with hot, soapy water and trod back to the fort, leaving the dogs in the house this time. When she reached the fort, the boys had picked up the trash. She handed Collin the large plastic bag. "Here, Collin, put all the garbage in this bag." She handed the bucket of water to Dalton and the rags to Benny. "Dalton, how about you and Benny wipe up the mess inside the fort."

The boys did a great job removing the trash and cleaning up the table and the floor of the fort. When they were finished, they resumed whatever activity had previously been interrupted.

Nora started back toward the house with the trash and the cleaning supplies. "Thanks, guys. Great job. Bet you'll be hungry for lunch soon."

When she reached the house, her cellphone rang just as she opened the French doors into the kitchen. "Hi, Amy."

"Hi, Mom. How are things going with the kids?"

"Oh, they seem to be enjoying themselves. I was just going to fix them some lunch. I had enough hot dogs and buns in the freezer. Sonya and I took them out this morning."

"Oh, good. Hope they all like hot dogs."

"We have the chips and snacks left over from the funeral. And Sonya and I made brownies. They should have plenty to eat."

Nora hesitated, wondering if she should tell Amy about the intruder. She didn't want her to worry, but then she decided she probably should mention it. "Oh, another thing. There's been a little excitement around here."

"What do you mean? What kind of excitement?"

45

Amy's tone sounded apprehensive.

"Someone was in the boy's fort sometime early this morning."

"Oh, my gosh! Did you call the police?"

"Calm down, Amy. It was probably some homeless person wanting to get out of the terrible storm we had last night."

"Mom, you don't know that. I'm calling the police."

"Don't be hasty. We already cleaned up the mess."

"You cleaned up the mess? What mess? What did this person do?"

"Oh, he just left some beer cans and cigarette butts lying around. That's all."

"Mom! This is serious. I'm calling the police, and I'm coming out. You'd better call the mothers of Sonya and Collin's friends and tell them to pick their kids up. They don't need to be around when the police arrive."

"Amy, aren't you overreacting? It was just a little mess. It didn't take long for the boys to clean it up."

"No, Mom. That's not the point. This is serious. You can't have a stalker out there while you, Sonya, and Collin are by yourselves. Those kind of creeps read the obituaries online and in the newspaper and sometimes target widows. They could've found out about you that way, thinking they could come to rob you. I have to call the police."

"Oh, I don't know. I don't think it was anything like that." But maybe Amy was right. It was probably best, just to be safe. "Okay, dear. Call the police. I'll get the kids to call their parents to pick them up."

Nora hung up, then phoned Sonya and Collin to come back to the house. A few minutes later, coming in the door, Collin looked around the kitchen. "Where's the food? I thought you called us for lunch, Granny."

"No, son. Sorry. Your friends need to go home. Your mom is calling the police about the intruder who was in the fort. She thinks it's best if everyone goes home. Maybe they can come back some other time. I'm so sorry."

"Aw, bummer!" moaned Collin.

Though they were disappointed, Dalton and Kyle called their mothers to pick up the kids. After they left, Nora quickly fixed a few hot dogs for Collin, Sonya, and herself while they waited for Amy and the police.

Chapter Five

Wednesday Afternoon

The police from Smith Township arrived mere seconds before Amy. She followed them up the walkway, talking to them while they approached the house. Nora opened the front door with Collin and Sonya directly behind her. Their eyes opened wide as they stared at the officers in their stiff, blue uniforms. Thank goodness, they've had very little experience with law enforcement in the past.

In the background the dogs started to bark. "Hey kids, how about putting the dogs in the utility room for now. Otherwise, it'll get too noisy to talk to the officers." Nora also wasn't sure how the dogs would react to the police. They too were never confronted by large men in uniforms before.

When the dogs had been confined, the two officers and Amy entered the house. Nora greeted them, "Hello, officers, Amy."

The tall, paunchy officer with the prickly looking face and bulbous nose introduced himself. "Ma'am, I'm Officer Gary McGuire and this is Officer Luke Graham."

Officer McGuire was the older of the two policemen—perhaps in his fifties—and seemed to be the one more in charge. Officer Graham was rugged looking and handsome.

"Come in, officers," Nora said. "Amy, you really didn't have to come out here. You're missing work."

"I know, but I want to find out what's going on."

After the introductions, Officer Graham asked, "I understand you had a home invasion last night?"

"Well, not exactly."

Nora told them about the condition of the fort. Then she told them about the broken doggie door and the flickering light she had seen in the woods.

Amy opened her mouth and stared at her mother. "Mom! You didn't tell me anything about those things?"

Nora glanced down at the floor. "Uh, I guess I also didn't tell you about the vehicle that rode my bumper and scared me half to death on the way back from Zep's Pizza last night."

"Oh, my gosh!" Amy protested. "What happened then?"

Nora described to Amy and the officers her harrowing experience in her minivan the night before. Officer Graham took notes while she recounted the incident. Then the officers checked out the doggie door before walking back into the woods to look at the fort. In the kitchen as Nora, Amy, and the kids waited for the officers to return, Amy gently clutched her mother's hand. "You should've told me about all this before."

"I didn't want to worry you. Anyhow, I don't think they're connected. The car was probably just kids out for a joy ride."

Sonya, who was leaning against the sink, stared at her grandmother with her wide eyes. "Granny, you didn't say anything to us last night about that either."

"Nothing bad happened, so I didn't want to worry you, honey."

Collin was frowning. "But you could've told us. Mom always says we should talk about things like this. Things that bother us. Right Mom?"

Shaking her head, Amy countered, "What about the intruder in the woods? That's definitely something to be concerned about. This is private property. No one should be on it without your permission."

"Oh, he was probably somebody wanting to get out of the rain. You know, it was really heavy last night."

Amy shook her head. "Mom, for some reason you're just making excuses. There's the broken doggie door too. How can you explain that?"

"Oh, probably some possum or raccoon or maybe a fox did that damage. We've had issues with them before."

Collin interjected, "Oh, wow! I wondered why the doggie door was all taped up."

Amy seemed very concerned. "I don't know, Mom. These can't all be coincidences. Maybe you should stay with Brian and Lisa after all until everything calms down."

Mouth slightly clenched, Nora shook her head. "You know that wouldn't be a good idea. I'd go crazy there."

Collin turned toward his mother. "Mom, we'll be all right. We'll look out for Granny."

Sonya added, "Yeah, Mom. You worry too much."

Amy glanced back and forth between the kids and her mother. Then she shook her head. Before she could say anything else, the police officers returned. "Looks like the fort was cleaned up. You should've left it so we could examine the evidence," advised Officer McGuire.

Nora nodded in agreement. "I guess you're right, but I didn't know we'd be calling the police today."

Amy addressed the officers. "So is there anything you can do to keep her safe? This place is far from neighbors and businesses. She's really on her own out here."

Officer McGuire tapped his lips with his forefinger. "We can have a patrol car come by at different intervals. I'd advise you, Mrs. Mitchell, to be sure all your windows and doors are locked. And if you notice any other suspicious or disturbing activity, don't hesitate to call 9-1-1 immediately."

Eyebrows raised, Amy stared at him. "That's it?"

"Well, ma'am, there's not much we can do at this point. No one entered the house, and nobody was actually harmed. As your mother said, these incidents might not even be connected." He turned toward Nora. "But if you have any other issues, be sure to call 9-1-1." With that, the officers left the house and drove away in their squad car.

Amy pleaded, "Oh, Mom. I don't like this at all. Maybe you should stay at the apartment with me and the kids."

"Don't be silly, Amy. The kids and I will be fine here. Your place is way too small for another person. I couldn't sleep on that pull-out couch of yours with my back the way it is."

"I'll sleep on the couch. You can sleep in my bed."

"No, no. I'm not going to take your bed. I'm staying here. We'll be fine. Right, kids?"

Collin put his hand on his mother's shoulder and gave her a reassuring look. "Mom, nothing really bad happened. We're having fun. And Granny said Dalton and Benny can come back next week. I didn't get a chance to show them everything to do around here. They didn't even get to go in the pool."

"Collin's right, Mom," agreed Sonya. "We want to stay. We haven't had a chance to do much of anything yet. You know how we are at home. Like you said, we get so bored."

Amy shook her head, put her hands up, and breathed a heavy sigh. "All right, all right. I guess I'm outnumbered here. You two are as stubborn as your grandmother."

Amy went back to work, and Nora and the kids spent most of the remainder of the afternoon in the pool. Nora tried not to think about any of the weird occurrences that had happened, and instead focused on enjoying her time with the kids.

For a while, Nora stayed in the pool with Sonya and Collin. However, the sun was a little too much for her aging skin even with a thick layer of sunscreen on her body. After a couple of hours, she dried off with her towel, wrapped it around herself, and sat on the screened porch, watching the kids as they played in the pool.

They really were good kids. Was that just a grandmother speaking? And Amy was such a good person. That wasn't just a mother talking. Anyone who knew Amy would agree. Yet her kindness and generosity hadn't always helped her make the best decisions in her life.

In high school, she belonged to a club whose purpose was to do humanitarian projects for the community. One of their projects was to collect food for the needy. With their social studies teacher as the chaperone, they delivered baskets of food to local churches, who would then dispense them to the disadvantaged members of their congregations.

One Saturday, the students took their baskets to Iglesia Vida Nueva, a small Spanish church on the north side of Youngstown. When the students arrived, a few of the teenage church members were renovating the sanctuary, painting the walls and repairing the pews. Carlos Suarez, one of those young men, saw Amy walk into the church with her blonde, curly hair and big blue eyes, carrying a huge basket of food. He immediately set his sights on her and hurried over to relieve her of the basket. She was tall, thin, and very noticeable, not like some of the short, stubby Mexican girls with whom he usually hung out.

As he took the basket from her, Amy also noticed dark, attractive Carlos, who looked nothing like boys she had formerly dated. She had recently broken up with Greg Nichols, who had been her steady boyfriend through most of her high school years. Now, in the beginning of her senior year, she was lonely and vulnerable. And this black-haired, bronze-skinned, deep brown-eyed, exotic Mexican lad welcomed her with open arms. Her parents tried to tell her that she and Carlos were not compatible.

Actually, Carlos wasn't a bad guy at all. It was just that he came from an entirely different culture from Amy's background. Of course, to a teenager, parents knew nothing. She was three months pregnant with Sonya when she graduated high school. She and Carlos got married, lived with Dave and Nora until they set the young family up in a small apartment on the west side of Youngstown. Dave got Carlos a job at the airport where he worked, and Amy did waitressing while Carlos' mother Mercedes watched Sonya.

Four years after Sonya was born, they welcomed Collin into the family. When he was a year old, Amy started taking night classes at Youngstown State to get an associate's degree in business administration. By then Carlos, who was a hard worker, became a foreman of his airport work crew. Eventually, Amy applied for an office manager position at the medical office of Dr. Bruno Petrakis, a heart surgeon in Austintown. She got the job and had worked for the doctor ever since.

Carlos and Amy's marriage began to fall apart shortly after Collin was born. Dave and Nora were not privy to the why's and how's of their disagreements. That was none of their business. Carlos and Amy's divorce was final when Collin started school. Amy moved with the kids to an apartment near her work, but the couple maintained joint custody of the children. However, Carlos was often remiss in his duty. When it was his turn to have the kids, he wasn't always around. Mercedes, who adored her grandchildren, would look after them. Nora believed that was why Collin was so close to Dave. He needed a father figure, though Nora felt Carlos' relationship with his children had changed the last few years. Amy told her that he took the kids on weekends quite often now. And the kids still saw Carlos' mother regularly.

Chapter Six

Wednesday Evening

The kids got out of the pool around six o'clock that evening. They were tired after the fort fiasco, the visit from the police, then spending the day under the hot afternoon sun.

"Do you guys want to go anywhere for dinner tonight?" Nora hoped they'd rather stay home.

On her way into the downstairs bathroom to change out of her swimsuit, Sonya replied, "I'd just as soon have the leftovers. That pizza was really good last night, and we didn't eat all of it."

"Me too," agreed Collin, while starting up the stairs to also change. "There's still some of the chicken left, too."

Thus, the three of them opted for leftovers again: pizza, chicken, salad, hot dogs, chips, and stale cookies. Nora needed to pitch all these leftovers soon.

After they ate and cleared the table, Collin suggested, "How about if we play some games? Do you still have them in the closet, Granny?"

"Good idea. Yes, they're still there. You choose the first one, and Sonya can choose the next one."

They played several board games for a couple of hours. Some of them even had Nora chuckling in spite of her maudlin mood. After a while, Sonya stood, stretching her long arms and arching her back. "I'm getting tired. I'm gonna shower and go to bed."

"Hey, you won the last game. You should give me a chance to win another one," challenged Collin.

"We'll play again tomorrow night, Collin. You don't want me to fall asleep on the board, do you?"

He snickered, "That'd be okay with me. Then I'd win for sure."

Sonya came over to hug Nora good night and traipsed up the stairs. Collin got out his phone and played a few games on it. Nora turned on the television and watched the evening news. About ten-thirty, Collin gave up too. "I'm gonna go to bed now, Granny. See you in the morning." He yawned and came over to give her a kiss and a hug.

Nora, of course, knew it would be useless to attempt sleep. She took a quick shower and put on her lightweight cotton pajamas and summer slippers. Back downstairs, she and the dogs gathered on the back porch to listen to Dave's sixties/seventies music CD again and feel sorry for herself some more.

Two of the dogs got comfortable in their usual spots: Amos at her feet and Gordy circling beside her at least ten times before settling into his position. However, Cleo again roamed the house searching for Dave before returning to the porch, looking at Nora with sorrowful eyes. She felt so bad for the dog. "Cleo, I know if you could talk, you'd ask me, 'Where is he? I can't find him?' I wish I could explain to you, but I can't even explain it to myself." Cleo stared at her for another minute or two before finally walking dejectedly to the stool on the other side of the porch. Even after she settled herself, Cleo continued to look longingly into the dark night beyond the screening.

Dave and Nora had acquired all three dogs as puppies but not all at the same time. Gordy, their champagne Pomeranian, was about six months old when they rescued him from the county dog pound after he was abandoned by his previous owner. Now he was about eleven. For a little old dog, he was in good health and very feisty. Maybe he'd keep Nora company for eleven more years. At least she could hope.

Cleo, the Doberman, was six. Being that the house was somewhat isolated, Dave wanted a good watchdog. When they brought Cleo home from the dog pound, she was just about three weeks old, too young to be without a mother. They also took her brother, Dodge, from the same litter. Someone had tossed them in a garbage barrel, and another person found them, dropping them off at the pound. Nora bottle fed the dogs, but sadly, Dodge didn't make it.

Dave and Nora found Amos, their black Lab, along the side of the road on one of their trips to the grocery store. Amos was about three months old, dirty and emaciated. They didn't get to the store that morning because they took him back home, bathed him, and treated him for the abundance of a flea population all over his body. When they fed him, he acted so hungry that Nora swore he didn't even breathe while he inhaled the food. After he drank a quart of water, he took a nap in the middle of the family room until the next morning. Cleo and Gordy constantly went over to him to sniff and check him out. At four, Amos was their baby.

Both Cleo and Amos definitely met the criteria for being great guard dogs. They were always alert to any strange or unusual occurrences in or around the house.

They immediately stiffened and focused with the hair on their backs standing up at the sound of any unusual noises. Nora had no doubt they'd attack anyone attempting to harm either Dave or herself, yet they were sweethearts with them, the grandkids, and any of their welcomed guests. Gordy was a bit hard of hearing these days. He didn't make a good watchdog anyhow because of his size. But like Nora often said, he sure could yap.

Chapter Seven

Late Wednesday Night

Deep in thought and reminiscing again, Nora must've been on the porch for an hour or more when she heard the doorbell ring. Shaking her head to clear her mind, she jerked upright and looked at her watch. The dogs, seeming confused, awakened suddenly and started to bark. A quarter till twelve! Who could that be at this hour of the night?

Perhaps it was the police officer who was supposed to drive by to keep an eye on the house. Nora wondered what he wanted, why he'd come to the door. Did he see something outside? She scuttled out of her seat and heard the doorbell ring again. She quickened her steps through the house so whoever it was wouldn't wake up the kids. She was still only in her pajamas and slippers with no robe. There was no time to go upstairs to get it. She assumed she'd simply need to check if it were the police officer and what he wanted. She wouldn't need to open the door completely for him.

Arriving at the door, she looked out the peep hole to see who it was so late at night. To her astonishment, the officer wasn't standing on the doorstep. Of all people, Sonya's friend, Deet, stood there, shifting his weight from side to side as if he had an urgent need to pee. *What the hell was he doing here?*

She unlocked the deadbolt and twisted the lock on the door handle. Opening the door just a crack, with a crinkled forehead and wide eyes, she stared at the kid. "Deet, what in heaven's name are you doing here? It's really late, and Sonya is asleep."

Deet seemed particularly nervous and didn't look directly at Nora, His eyes shifted in all directions. "Can I talk to Sonya, Mrs. Mitchell?"

"She's in bed. I don't want to wake her at this hour. What is so important you have to talk to her tonight? How come you didn't call or text her? I'm sure you have her phone number." She paused and looked behind him. "How did you even get here?"

Deet seemed even more flustered as he wiped his forehead with his forearm. "It's about Kyle. Something terrible has happened. Please. Can I come in?"

"Oh, my God! What happened? Is he okay?"

The dogs softly growled behind her. They had only briefly met Deet earlier that day. Plus, they weren't used to visitors coming to the house that late at night. They were usually in doggie dreamland by at least ten o'clock. Since Sonya had introduced him to Nora earlier, Deet was not a complete stranger to her. Still, she felt uneasy.

Before she had a chance to make up her mind to either close the door on Deet or open it, the decision was made for her. In one split second, like an explosion, the door burst open, wrenching her hand attached to the door handle. Pain shot up her arm like a firecracker. The flying door hit her forehead, causing her to tumble to the floor nearly on top of Gordy, who quickly scampered out of the way.

Everything happened fast, yet it seemed to go in

slow motion. While Cleo and Amos went wild, Nora lay on the floor. From the corner of her eye she saw three large men dressed completely in black, standing before her. They wore long pants and long-sleeved shirts, with full, stark white masks covering their entire faces. Black stocking caps concealed their heads. They had barged through the open doorway. One stepped on the calf of Nora's leg while another scrunched her hair close to her scalp, nearly stepping on her head. As she screeched in pain, Cleo and Amos lunged at the dark figures. The strangers knocked the dogs away, but not before Cleo latched on to one of their legs and Amos bit into another man's arm.

Then Nora heard a thud and an almost simultaneous loud yelp from Amos. At the same time, she also heard the sound of footsteps scurrying down the stairs accompanied by screams. "Granny! Granny!"

In all this confusion, a gruff voice yelled, "Hold it right there. Don't come any closer."

As Nora tried to climb off the floor, Sonya, bare-footed and still in her T-shirt and boxer shorts, screamed again, "Granny!"

Collin, also still in bare feet, T-shirt, and boxers and paying no attention to the voice telling him to halt, came over and helped Nora stand up. Sonya immediately joined him, grabbing Nora's other arm. "Are you okay, Granny?"

Shaking her throbbing hand and then rubbing her head where her hair was torn from her scalp, Nora was stunned and in pain but not seriously hurt. While the kids held onto her from each of her sides, the three of them tried to back away from the intruders, but the masked men each seized and immobilized them.

The same gruff voice spoke again. "Listen up, douche bags. Here's what you're gonna do. You three"—he kept Nora in his grip and motioned toward the kids—"you're gonna go into that room, sit on the couch while I tell you what you'll do next."

The three intruders shoved them forward. Nora, Sonya, and Collin, upset and shocked, stumbled toward the living room. But the dogs were not cooperating as well as the humans. They continued to leap and snap at the men. The man holding onto Nora tossed his head toward Collin. "You! Shorty! Do somethin' with those mutts before I kill 'em."

Collin murmured, "I'm gonna need help. They won't come with me willingly."

Sonya twisted loose from her captor, picked up Gordy and pulled at Cleo's collar, leading them back to the utility room.

Amos had blood oozing from his nose where one of the intruders had punched him. As he led Amos away, Collin snarled, "I'm gonna clean his wound first."

The number one man said nothing as the dogs were taken away. When Sonya and Collin walked toward the kitchen, one of the other men followed them and pulled out a gun from his waistband, pointing it at their backs.

In a daze, Nora staggered to the couch. So much had taken place in the span of just a couple of minutes she couldn't think straight. She couldn't wrap her mind around what was happening. She kept staring at the two remaining men wearing the white masks and stocking caps on their heads despite the warm May weather. And she looked over at Deet, who did nothing but stand apart from everyone, chewing on his fingernails and breathing heavily as if he were watching some scary movie. He had not participated in any of the violence.

When the kids returned from confining the dogs, they sat on the couch, one on each side of Nora. The dogs still wildly barked and howled even though the door to the utility room was closed tightly. The man who had followed them to the utility room went over to stand next to the other man a few feet away from the main man but looking directly at those on the couch. Deet still appeared extremely nervous while standing next to those two men. The tyrant making all the demands paced back and forth in front of the couch, erratically waving and pointing a gun at Nora and the kids.

Sonya looked at Deet. "Hey, dude, what's going on? Why are you doing this?"

Deet peered at her with watery, wide eyes, but before he said a word, the number one guy moved close to Sonya. "You! No talking." As he came close to her and put his face directly in front of Sonya's, despite the mask Nora whiffed his foul breath seeping through the mouth hole. Odor also reeked from the armpits of his sweaty, dark shirt. They had to be extremely hot in their black outfits and smothering masks. Certainly, not any concern of hers.

"Now, let's get one thing straight," the main guy bellowed. "You're not to open your mouths unless you're given permission. You are to remain seated unless one of us gives you a task to do." His fierce eyes scanned over the three hostages on the couch as he yelled, "Is that clear?"

Nora nodded her head. Sonya defiantly stared at the man. As Nora feared, Collin, who often had a tendency to question authority, decided to speak. He was polite about it, anyhow. "Sir, what do you want? Why are you he—"

Before Collin finished his question, the man forcibly slapped him across the face. Collin's cheek immediately turned bright pink and swelled to twice its size.

Okay. Nora was obeying this man so he wouldn't hurt anyone. But he had no call to slap her grandson. She bounded off the couch. "Listen, mister, we'll do what you ask, but don't you dare hurt my grandchildren."

The man's answer came as a surprise. He suddenly pushed her back onto her seat.

Then both Collin and Sonya leaped off the couch. The other two men rushed toward them, one grabbing Collin, twisting his arm behind his back. The other clasped Sonya around the waist and threw her onto the carpet.

Mayhem broke loose. Kicking, punching, scratching, biting, and screaming. Nora jumped up and threw a fist at the main guy's face while ducking her head as he tried to bat her away. The punch only nipped him in the jaw. All the while, in the background, the dogs barked and howled incessantly, scratching frantically at the utility room door, trying unsuccessfully to escape and come to their rescue.

Eventually the intruders, being more powerful, wrestled Nora, Sonya, and Collin back to the couch. In the tussle, Sonya had torn off the mask of her assailant, making his face visible to everyone. His skin was tawny, and a two-day beard spotted his chin. His wide, pugged nose looked like it had once been broken. His eyes were deep set and appeared a bit closer together than normal. As far as she knew, Nora had never seen him before. On his cheek, a deep scratch dripped blood. He removed a white handkerchief from his pants pocket and dabbed at the wound, glancing at the bloody handkerchief with each dab.

Breathing heavily, Sonya looked rebellious, yet satisfied as she victoriously stared at the bleeding man.

Deet had migrated to a corner of the room and sat helplessly on the floor, clasping his knees up to his chest. He whimpered like a wounded animal. He had not played any part in the recent debacle.

The number one man was definitely not handling the situation in any way similar to Deet. His anger exploded from his body. Nora hoped Sonya and Collin would remain quiet so he wouldn't be upset any more than he was already. She also needed to take her own advice.

The man kept waving the handgun in front of the trio on the couch as he paced back and forth. He was out of control, breathing heavily with spittle coming out of the mouth hole in his mask. He passed by Sonya, moved to stand in front of Nora, and pressed the gun hard against her forehead. She cringed as she felt the cold pressure of the metal gun barrel.

The man's entire body shook as the gun gently danced against Nora's forehead. She feared he might accidently, if not on purpose, pull the trigger. He was a madman. "Look what you've done, you stupid asses!" he shrieked. "Look what you've done! You've provoked me and caused me to lose my temper. I don't like to be provoked. I don't like to lose my temper." Then he removed the gun from Nora's head, stood perfectly still, and suddenly laughed maniacally. "There will be consequences."

No doubt, he was infuriated with his captives, but Nora was just as enraged as he was. Her head throbbed where she'd crashed into the door. Her wrist ached from being twisted off the door handle. Her scalp burned from where chunks of hair were yanked out. Her injured leg from being kicked when they entered *her* house was swelling up like a balloon. For the sake of the kids, she didn't mention these grievances to this maniac. She saw Collin rubbing his arm where the second man had twisted it. Sonya had a large bruise puffing up the left side of her face, which she apparently got from the man with the bleeding scratch on his cheek.

They were in a dire predicament at the mercy of three incontrollable madmen.

After the number one man calmed down somewhat, he began to lecture them again. "You know you assholes have spoiled everything. No one had to get hurt. Now look what you've done." He continued pacing, stopping in front of each of them as he pivoted by the couch.

He jerked his head toward Deet. "Hey, wimp. Get over here."

Deet jumped out of the corner and trotted to the number one man. His entire body trembled. "Yeah, dude. Whatchu want me to do?"

"First, grow up, kid! I want you to act like a man instead of crawling into the corner like a scared rabbit. Then I want you to find something to tie these assholes up so they can't cause any more problems. If they were a nice little family, this wouldn't be necessary. All they had to do was cooperate and listen to me. We could get what we came for and be on our merry way." He stopped in front of Nora. "But no, you had to be cute, didn't you?"

He turned and walked away, then in two steps was back in her face with his rancid breath making her want to puke. He shouted so loud her ears rang. "Hey, old woman, where do you keep rope or duct tape?"

She shook her head to get her hearing back, and she grinned at him slyly. "You aren't very well prepared, young man. Why didn't you bring your own restraints if you knew you were going to invade my home?"

Her sass was not what he wanted to hear. He squinted his eyes, stooped so near to her that his lips were at kissable distance from Nora's. Talk about nausea: If she would vomit, it would go right into that hole in his mask. Ugh! He placed the gun against her forehead for a second time. She stiffened as she again felt the cold metal cutting into her skin. Spittle spewed through the hole of the mask, some landing on her chin.

"Listen, old bitch. I've had about enough of your attitude. Where is the damn tape or the damn rope?"

She tipped her head to the side so his gun no longer pressed on her head and his lips couldn't discharge his putrid breath onto her mouth. "They're in the utility room where the dogs are being held captive."

The man stood upright. Moving the gun away, he darted his eyes from side to side. Then he suddenly grabbed Nora's arm at the shoulder and pulled her from the couch. "You go with him. And, Deet, if she tries anything funny, punch her in the face." He gave her a firm shove toward the boy.

She was surprised he didn't have one of his cronies with a gun follow her instead of Deet, who had no weapon. Maybe he was smart enough to realize she wouldn't try anything foolish while her grandkids were held at gunpoint. If that was what he thought, he was correct. This wasn't the time or the opportunity to find a way out of this horrible nightmare.

With Deet following her toward the kitchen, she had to see if she could get some answers from this scared kid. He was acting as if he wanted no part of this mess. Yet he was the reason she had opened the front door in the first place. "Deet, what's going on here? What have you gotten us into?"

Deet was actually crying and trembling. "Mrs. Mitchell, honest, I didn't know they were gonna hurt you guys. Sonya's my friend. I wouldn't do anything to harm her."

"Well, maybe you wouldn't, but these 'friends' of yours who have invaded my house don't have the same inclination as you do. If Sonya is your friend, why would you lead those men here?"

"It's a long story, ma'am. Believe me. I didn't know they were gonna hurt anybody."

They were at the utility room door. "Okay, Deet, but I'll expect a decent explanation from you when you get a chance. Otherwise, if we get out of this situation, you are in serious trouble."

She carefully opened the door to avoid allowing the dogs to escape. Panting and jumping, they gathered around her. She quickly patted each of them on the head and briefly petted them, calmly saying words to try consoling them. "It's okay, doggies. It's okay." She surely didn't want them to receive any further abuse or injuries from those monsters. She turned to Deet. "You wait outside while I get the tape."

"Uh, I'd better not, ma'am. It's not that I don't trust you, but if there's anything in there you can use as a weapon, Primo will kill you and me both if he finds it on you."

Her hand froze while she petted Amos. Did she hear him right? Did he just give her that main guy's name? Primo?

As she continued to calm the dogs and keep them away from Deet, she casually asked, "Primo, huh? Is that the boss-man's name?"

"Oh, shit! What've I done? Now he'll kill me for sure. Please, please, don't let him know I said his name. I'm beggin' you. Seriously, he'll kill me."

She walked over toward the cabinet where she kept the duct tape. "Okay, Deet. I won't tell him, but you have to promise me you'll explain how you're mixed up in all this mess."

"Yes, ma'am. First chance I get. Yes, ma'am."

"First chance you get. Or else." She wasn't sure what she actually meant by "or else".

She retrieved a couple of rolls of duct tape from the tall, gray cabinet. What a coincidence! She probably hadn't used this tape in years. And here she was, twice in the same day. First to bind the doggie door, and now to bind her and her grandchildren.

She hugged and petted the dogs once more, and she and Deet snuck back out the door as swiftly as possible. The dogs began to whine and scratch at the door immediately when they walked away. Poor things. They were so upset, all cooped up in that small room. During the funeral, they were confined in there for hours. And now, while strangers roamed in *their* house causing havoc, once more they were prisoners.

Once outside the utility room, Nora handed the rolls of tape to Deet, who carried them back to the living room. Primo still paced in front of Collin and Sonya. This man was really a nervous, impatient, and unpredictable creature. Nora had to watch him carefully and treat him cautiously. She had to be aware and vigilant.

"Hey!" Primo turned to the other men, who jumped to attention. "Get three chairs from that dining room and bring them in here. Move it!"

The two men and Deet darted into the dining room, and each grabbed a chair, carrying them into the living room and setting them in the center of the room facing the couch.

"Bind them up," Primo ordered.

Deet gently pulled Sonya off the couch. Giving him a venomous look, she yanked her arm from his grasp before plopping herself on one of the recently positioned chairs.

Wanting to be in the middle of the kids in hopes she might get an opportunity to communicate with them, Nora rose from the couch on her own and walked herself to the center chair. Collin stood and crossed the room to sit on the final chair.

Just as these goons were about to restrain them, the doorbell rang. Nora came off the chair like a shot. *Now what? Who could that be?*

Everyone stopped what they were doing. Primo stared at Nora. "Who the hell is that?"

"I don't know. Seems like I'm getting all kinds of interesting visitors tonight."

"All right, smartass. Go see who it is. And get rid of them. You know what'll happen if you don't." He pointed his gun at the kids.

He motioned to the bare-faced man. "Go follow her, and if she does anything stupid, shoot her and whoever is at the door."

The bare-faced man grabbed Nora's arm and pulled her in front of him. He pushed her toward the entrance hall, and she stumbled before catching her balance, at the same time trying to think how she could alert the new visitor to the calamity going on inside the house.

At the door, she looked through the peep hole. A police officer stared back at her.

Great! How do I make him aware of the situation? Or do I send him away?

She flicked on the porch light and partially opened the door. "Hello, officer. Is something wrong?" She hoped the officer didn't notice the shakiness in her voice.

The policeman responded immediately. "Ma'am, Officer McGuire assigned me to check up on you. Is everything okay?"

Damn! Everything was *not* all right. But how could she convey this to the officer? She didn't want to endanger Sonya and Collin's lives by confessing what was taking place as they spoke. She also felt she'd be risking her life and the policeman's since the bare-faced man was holding a gun on her. So she made a snap decision. She lied.

"Uh, yes, officer. Everything is fine." She hoped her voice didn't sound as strange to him as it did to her.

"Well, ma'am, I noticed a black van in front of your garage that wasn't here earlier when I came down your drive. Are you sure you're okay?"

More lies. "Oh, uh, that's my... that's my son's van. He decided to stay with me a couple of days. Uh, it's probably no longer necessary for you to check on us any longer. We'll be okay with him here. Thank you so much, officer." *Liar, liar, pants on fire.*

"Are you sure, ma'am? It's no problem for us."

"Yes. I'm sure we'll be fine with my son here. Thanks again for stopping by."

The officer walked away but stopped at his cruiser's door and looked back at Nora before entering his car. She waved to him and smiled. He got in his vehicle, turned around in the drive, and drove away.

Gone was their chance for freedom.

As soon as Nora walked back into the living room with the bare-faced man's gun still focused on the middle of her back, Primo badgered, "Who the hell was it, bitch?"

She sat on the chair between Sonya and Collin without looking at the brute. "It was the police officer assigned to check up on us since some crazy-ass hoodlums were in my woods last night, stalking us."

She wasn't sure it that statement was true, but if looks could kill... However, they can't, and Primo didn't say anything after her taunting remark. He simply addressed his cronies. "Okay, let's get these fine folks tied up so we can get down to business."

Still, Nora needed to watch her tongue with this man. He was so unpredictable. But sometimes she just couldn't control what came out of her mouth. Dave was the diplomat. Not her. He'd often warned her about her cynical demeanor—one day it would get her in trouble.

The crony with the mask on took the duct tape

from Deet and got behind Collin. He grabbed Collin's arms and roughly twisted them around the chair. He was about to unwind the tape and wrap it around Collin's hands when he unexpectedly stopped. Looking bewildered, he asked Primo, "How'm I gonna cut this?"

Primo turned toward him, let out a deep puff of air, and shook his head. "Dumbass! Go in the kitchen and get a knife. What's wrong with you? Don't you know anything?"

Primo was irritated with everyone. Nora didn't know how dangerous he actually was, but by the sounds of his voice and by the way he swung that gun around, she didn't want to take any chances of finding out.

The man he called dumbass handed the tape to the bare-faced man and went into the kitchen. He came back with one of Nora's knives and set it on a nearby table.

The bare-faced man had already pulled Nora's arms behind the back of the chair. He twisted her hands together so tightly they were already getting numb from lack of circulation. She winced but said nothing as he wrapped the tape three times firmly around her wrists. Taking the knife from the table, he cut the tape and handed the roll to Deet.

Deet took the tape but held it for several seconds while he stood staring at Sonya's back. Primo glared at him. "Well, kid, do you think that tape is gonna magically roll around that bitch's wrists all by itself?"

Deet moved closer toward Sonya, gently grabbed her arms, and brought them around the chair. He bound her wrists, cut the tape with the knife, and passed the knife and the tape back to the guy with his mask still on. For lack of a better name, Nora decided to use the name Primo called him—Dumbass.

Dumbass grabbed Collin's arms and twisted them behind the chair again. Collin grimaced as the man roughly pulled them together. Dumbass wound the tape around Collin's wrists several times, and then he grabbed the knife to cut the tape. In the process, he nicked Collin's wrist. Blood oozed out of the small cut. Collin cried out, "Ow! Take it easy, dude."

No sooner had he finished his sentence when Primo jumped in front of Collin and slapped him across the face again. "Hey, you little twerp. I said no talking!"

That was the last straw! Nora's temper took over. She wriggled to stand up, pulling the chair with her and stumbling toward Primo. She stood in front of him with the chair stuck to her back. "I don't know who you think you are or what you want from us. We're trying to cooperate, but you're making it very difficult. I'm telling you once again. Do not hurt my grandchildren, or you will get no cooperation whatsoever from me. And whatever you want from us, I promise you won't get it!"

Primo stood at least a head taller than her. He dropped his gun arm to his side. He said nothing at first, just nodded his head. Then he shook his head in disgust. "Listen, you old bitch. You don't tell *me* what to do here. You sit your wrinkled old ass back down and shut your friggin' mouth before I really get angry."

He gave Nora's forehead a hard shove; both she and her chair staggered back between Collin and Sonya, the chair quavering before it settled on all four legs.

Okay. Maybe she got the message this time. No use aggravating this crazy tyrant any further. They had to be careful. First, they needed to find out exactly what his plans were. She knew they were there for money. Why didn't they just rob her and leave them alone? They could be out of there by now and escape before law enforcement could even get to her property. And that's what worried her. Although she didn't recognize him, they already saw one of the intruders' faces. Now she also knew this bully's name. Not sure if it was a nickname, his first name, or his last name. Whatever, it was a way to identify him. None of this was good. She had to think, and their current circumstances didn't make that very easy.

The men and Deet bound the captives' legs to their chairs and pushed them about a foot apart so they couldn't touch each other. After the last confrontation, Nora hoped the kids knew not to speak again. She also hoped she'd have the sense to stop any more of her reproachful and snide remarks. But sometimes she couldn't control herself. Just like Dave always said— her temper was one thing he both loved and hated about her, depending upon whom it was focused.

When they were completely immobilized, Primo plopped his body onto the couch and widely splayed his arms and legs. He motioned to the other hooligans. "Sit."

With the gun still in his hand but resting beside him on the couch, his eyes scanned back and forth over the three captives in front of him. "Now, old woman, we're gonna get down to business. Here's what you're gonna do for me."

Chapter Eight

When She Was Young

Nora couldn't say she never was subjected to a dangerous situation before those monsters invaded her home. When a person lived as long as she had lived, there was bound to be something in her life that caused her heart to beat extra fast and fear to encompass her being. Something she'd remember the rest of her life. Yes, there was the other night when that car followed her in the rain. Although she wasn't positive, she considered that incident part and parcel of the whole crime spree of Primo and his cronies at her expense. She would think of it that way until it was proven otherwise.

There were also incidents when she was a kid that scared her half to death. Like the time Nora, her brother Donny, and her best friend Nancy snuck inside this beat-up, old house they *thought* was abandoned until the owner in his underwear came out of a bedroom brandishing a two-foot-long shotgun. They hightailed it out of there like a bat out of hell. Luckily, the man didn't shoot his gun at them. Nora heard gunshots when they ran across the front of his property, but she thought he was shooting into the air. She was so afraid that she peed her pants before they made it home.

Or the time her cousin, Jerry Chambers, took her

and Donny to search for "The Green Man" in Beaver County, Pennsylvania, about seventy miles from Youngstown. Jerry and his girlfriend, Judy, were babysitting Nora and her brother on this cold Saturday night in October while her parents attended some office party. She had heard the tale of The Green Man and wanted to see him for herself to discover if he was for real or a scary myth. The legend claimed that a man— or perhaps a ghost—with iridescent green skin and pitch-black holes where his eyes and nose should be would stalk the area late at night, dragging his booted feet along the deserted road. As soon as her parents left for the party, she convinced Jerry to drive to where The Green Man allegedly did his haunting on Route 351. When they arrived about an hour and a half later, Jerry's car was not the only one at the haunting site. Probably about a half dozen other cars were parked along the roadside. Jerry pulled over on the berm, and they waited like the other people, hoping to get a peek at The Green Man if he appeared.

Lo and behold, about twenty minutes later, a figure emerged from the dense woods. Nora couldn't believe her eyes. Everything she had heard about this man, not a ghost, was true. He *was* greenish looking, and he had holes for his eyes and nose. But the weird thing about seeing this poor man—she wasn't afraid of him like she expected to be. She didn't scream in terror, freak out, or hide her eyes. Instead, she was sad, so emotional that she cried and whimpered to Jerry, "Oh, Jerry, please. Let's go. That poor man!" She felt so sorry for him that she wanted to leave immediately. As a kid, it was painful to even look at his broken body and distorted face.

Several years ago, Nora was curious about what happened to The Green Man. She looked up the true story of him on the internet. His actual name was Raymond Robinson, who at nine years old was injured by an electrical line when he climbed a pole to get to a bird's nest. He was electrocuted and fell to the ground. As a result, he became severely disfigured and lost both eyes, his nose, and his right arm. After the accident, because of his appearance, he rarely ventured outside during the daytime. Instead, he would walk at night along Route 351, keeping one foot on the pavement and one on the grass and carrying a stick to help guide his way. Sometimes the teenagers who came to see him would give him beer or cigarettes. Some of them were not friendly and would taunt and tease him, many throwing stones at him. Several times he was hit by passing cars. Per Nora's research, in 1985 Raymond Robertson died at the age of seventy-five in a geriatric facility in Beaver County. Such a sad, sad story: actually, not a story but somebody's wretched life.

Another event in Nora's youth was the most terrifying of all. It will also be stuck in her memory forever. Very frightening but very different.

Nora, Donny, and her parents were on vacation in North Carolina and went white water rafting on the Nantahala River. She was twelve and Donny was ten. The intensity level of the rapids was only mild to moderate. Plus, the part of the river they were approaching purportedly wasn't too deep or rugged. Nora wasn't sure what happened when they entered this particular set of rapids.

Besides her family, five other people were in the raft: the guide, a student at the University of North

Carolina in Ashville on summer break; a young couple on their honeymoon, probably in their twenties; a heavyset man about sixty or so, very out of shape; and another man, muscular and fit, probably in his forties and wearing a bright red shirt.

The rafters had no issues until their raft started over this certain set of rapids. Everyone was doing as the guide instructed, although the heavyset man seemed a bit out of breath. The raft stayed upright, and they were doing okay paddling and steering through the swift and jarring waters. Nora could see ahead where the river seemed to stop in the middle of the sky. Suspecting it was a waterfall, she assumed it wasn't going to be too much of a drop to the river below. After all, this part of the river was not supposed to be dangerous, and their guide didn't give them any special instructions or precautions.

Just before they started over the falls, their raft hit a huge, floating log, and the raft capsized, sending everyone into the cold river water. At first Nora was enjoying her predicament. She swallowed a little fishy tasting water, no big deal. The raft had righted itself at the bottom of the falls, and after coming to the surface, she was able to grab onto it and pull herself on board again. Her parents, the young couple, the red-shirted man, and the guide quickly swam toward the raft and climbed on right after Nora. They were exhilarated and hyped from their drenching in the water and their trip over the falls. It wasn't until they were all on board that they realized Donny and the heavyset man weren't with them. Her father and the young guide immediately jumped back into the water to search for her brother and the missing man.

Her mother became a basket case. She kept leaning over the side of the raft. "Donny! Donny! Where are you? Please come up! Please!"

Nora thought her mother would fall back into the water. "Come on, Mom. They'll find him," she pleaded, trying to pull her away from the edge. But her mother shrugged Nora off and continued to yell for Donny.

It seemed like an eternity but was probably only a minute or two before those on the raft saw Nora's dad finally breaking through the water and dragging Donny over the side of the raft. Her mom screamed and cried all at the same time while her dad placed Donny on the floor of the raft and began CPR on him. Her mom kept yelling, "Come on, Donny. Breathe! Come on, baby."

Nora felt so helpless. There they were in the middle of the river with no one around to assist them, and the guide and the old man hadn't come out of the water yet.

Finally, Donny started choking and spitting up water. Her father turned him on his side so the water wouldn't go back down his throat.

About the same time, the guide emerged from the water. He had a look on his face Nora will never forget. Defeat. Fear. Sadness. The old man wasn't with him.

The guide instructed, "Come on, everyone. Paddle the raft to the shore. I'll get help." His walkie-talkie had been affixed to the raft in a waterproof container. He removed it and called his base to report the accident. Within fifteen minutes, the riverbank was inundated with people: rescuers, paramedics, police, and river authorities. Nora's mother accompanied Donny to the hospital in an ambulance while she and her dad followed them in the back of a police vehicle.

The next day Donny told his family what he remembered. "After I fell into the water, I tried to swim back to the top, but I felt some kind of heavy weight land on top of me. That big man had crashed into me, crushing my arm against a pointed rock on the river bed. You know, that fat man didn't even move as I tried to push him off me. I guess he had a heart attack or was unconscious for some reason. Pretty soon I blacked out, but somehow I felt the man's body floating away from me. I don't remember anything else until I started coughing my guts out and seeing everybody staring at me with scary lookin' eyes." Later, Donny learned that his dad and the guide had jumped in the water to rescue him and pull him onto the raft.

Donny was in the hospital overnight. He had broken his arm in several places. It still gave him trouble as an adult. Everyone was amazed how her father and the guide were able to move that poor man off Donny. However, Nora never learned just how the man actually died.

Yes, that was a very upsetting experience for Nora's family. None of them would ever forget it. And now, different time, different family members, and different adversary. It wasn't a river in North Carolina but three thugs trying to create havoc in their lives, in her own home. And doing a hell of a good job of it.

Chapter Nine

Early Thursday Morning

Primo slouched like a king on the couch, resting against the back, arms and legs spread wide, staring at Nora, Sonya, and Collin. They stared back at him but remained silent for fear of further retributions.

Nora surmised it was about three in the morning by then. Lack of sleep made her tired, lightheaded, and cranky. She and the kids each had some kind of injury, nothing major but still irritating and painful. She worried especially about Collin's arm after it was twisted so hard behind his back. He wasn't crying, but his eyes were glassy with moisture that could descend his cheeks at any second.

Primo bolted upright on his seat and focused his attention on Nora. "Old woman, you and these two brats have a job to do. You're gonna find me every single bit of money in this house wherever it is: purses, wallets, drawers, safes, and even under mattresses. That goes for any classy jewelry and electronics. That'll be your first task. You'll be followed by one of my men. After that, you'll come back here while my men search the house to make sure you didn't neglect to find some hidden cash or anything else valuable. If they find you 'accidentally forgot' some of these things, someone will be punished."

His intense eyes stared diabolically at the trio. "Maybe you!" he bellowed and pointed to Collin, who jerked his head to attention. "Maybe you!" He pointed to Sonya, who turned her head sideways to avoid looking at him. "Or maybe you, old woman." He pointed to Nora. She didn't move but looked directly into his demonic eyes.

Primo sat back on the couch where he continued his rant. "Because you didn't behave, we had to strap you to these chairs. All that work, right? But I can't trust you, can I?"

Another pause and a visual scan of the three captives. "What I'm gonna do is release this boy first." He motioned toward Collin by waving his left hand while shaking his extended index finger. "Kid, you go through the entire house, finding money, jewelry, anything worth money, wherever you can."

He then pointed at Sonya. "After your bratty brother returns with all our booty, you do the same as he did. I'm sure he doesn't know all your hiding places. You have some special things you hide from this old woman, don't you? Maybe where you keep those fancy little lacey panties of yours. I'm sure my friends here would like to see some of those frilly little things. Or maybe where you keep your weed that Deet gave you." He chuckled and looked at Dumbass and the one Nora called Bareface for lack of a better name.

Sonya, fuming like a mad bull ready to charge, stared at Primo. But she kept her cool and said nothing, just focused her attention on Primo with her chin up and her lips tightly pursed. Nora tried to give her an understanding glance, but Sonya didn't look her way. Then Primo turned his attention to Deet, who was still trembling on the other side of the room. "Deet, my boy, wouldn't you like to watch this little chickie look into her silky panty drawer? Maybe she'll model them for you and strip down to her naked ass. How would you like that?" Primo came forward on the couch, roaring in laughter while Deet continued looking at the floor.

Sonya still said nothing, but Nora knew her granddaughter well. She was seething inside. Her eyes remained doggedly focused on Primo, the hatred in them trying to burst out. If looks could kill...

Until this point, Nora hadn't even considered any sexual violence from these thugs. She surmised they were simply there for money and whatever else worth stealing. She even had a slim hope the three of them would get out of this with limited injuries. Sure, these thieves would take her valuables and her money, but that was just stuff, nothing else. In the scheme of things, money and stuff were insignificant. However, she now realized she was being naive. After Primo's latest remarks, she changed her mind.

No doubt, these loathsome creatures planned to seize everything she owned. But now she sensed they were capable of *anything*. Now she worried they might consider raping Sonya or, who knows, maybe even Collin. It was possible those vile men would stop at nothing to get what they wanted. Somehow, she had to find a way to thwart their plans before it was too late.

Primo looked at Collin. "You're gonna be first. You find what you can and come back here so we can give your sweet sissy and your old grandma a chance to find the big stuff." His voice took on a menacing, authoritative tone as he fixated on Sonya and Nora. "Nod your heads if you understand."

Like school children, all three nodded obediently but definitely not with happy, childlike faces.

Primo was quiet for a few moments, looking at each of his captives individually. Nora didn't want to think what was going on inside that twisted mind. Without warning, he jumped up and signaled to Dumbass. "Get over here. Take the kid to find the loot."

With difficulty, Dumbass unbound Collin's feet and struggled unsuccessfully with the tape on the boy's hands. When Primo got impatient, he yelled, "What the hell? Cut it off, stupid. Thanks to the old hag, we have plenty of tape."

Collin cringed and jerked as Dumbass used the knife on the tape. When he finally stood and brought his hands to the front, he realized he had been cut once again. Blood splattered from his wrist as he shook his hands to increase their circulation. Nora had to put an end to this madness before these monsters went too far.

Too far?

They'd already gone way beyond that point.

Collin left the room with Dumbass pointing a gun at his back. They came out of the kitchen with Collin carrying a few tall, white, plastic kitchen bags. He hesitated and looked into the living room, then they went toward the stairs.

All was quiet as the others sat in the living room. Deet flopped on a chair near the doorway to the dining room with his eyes cast downward. Primo continued the slouched posture on the couch, the same satisfied look in his eyes. Bareface stood patiently watching Nora and Sonya with his intense eyes. Sonya and Nora sat awaiting their turn to raid the house of Nora's possessions. Every once in a while, Nora heard footsteps through the ceiling as Collin and Dumbass searched the various rooms upstairs. They were up there for what seemed like hours but was probably about ten or fifteen minutes. When they came downstairs, Collin stood at the doorway to the living room. While holding a bulging kitchen bag in his right hand, he raised his left hand high into the air and waved it to get Primo's attention.

Primo looked at him. "What do you want, twerp?"

Collin put down his hand. "Should I check in the utility room? The dogs might get upset again."

"You think I care if those friggin' animals *get upset*? Got anything in there worth something?"

"I don't know. I was just gonna check."

"Well do it then. To hell with those dogs. If they make too much noise, I'll shoot 'em."

Looking upset with Primo's threat, Collin took in a deep breath, letting it out slowly as he made a sharp pivot toward the kitchen to do what he was ordered. When he opened the utility room door, the dogs began to bark and whine. He quieted them down somehow while he searched the room, and the noise ceased for a few minutes. However, the dogs' howling began again when Collin opened the door to leave.

While Collin stayed in the kitchen, Nora heard sounds of cabinet doors opening and closing, dishes clinking against each other, cutlery being moved around, and pots and pans banging. It sounded like he was doing a very thorough job. She wondered in what shape the kitchen would be when he was done. She wasn't concerned, for she had more important things to worry about.

Then she heard the French doors opening onto the

back porch. She had nothing of value out there. Those jerks wouldn't be interested in her plants—maybe if they were marijuana. Did they have a strong desire to read old newspapers and magazines stacked on the bottom shelf of the end table? How about dirty pillows on which the dogs slobbered, slept, and wiped their butts? Dave's set of weights were out there. Dumbass looked a little tubby around his middle. He could probably put them to use.

Who the hell knew what they thought was valuable? Who the hell cared? Nora just wished they'd take what they wanted and leave her and her grandkids alone.

Collin came back into the living room with Dumbass close behind. He carried one kitchen bag filled to the brim; Dumbass wielded another. They set them in front of Primo. Moving to an open area of the room, Primo dumped both bags onto the floor. He put his hands on his hips and sneered down at the pile, nudging the items with his foot.

Collin had selected things *he* thought were important. Apparently, most of them weren't too impressive to Primo. He began picking up items and tossing them into a vacant corner of the room: computer games; Collin's new shoes and suit he had worn to the funeral; some tools he found in the utility room; a couple of Hummel figurines—which broke when a heavy hammer landed on them—that came from Nora's bedroom; and various other items a kid might think were valuable. As for the Hummels, those particular figurines had been worth a few hundred dollars each— before they were broken. Primo's loss. Maybe *he* should be called Dumbass.

Primo picked up Collin's wallet from the pile. He opened it and withdrew the cash from the bill section. There wasn't much, a five dollar bill and a few singles. He waved them at Collin. "High roller, aren't you, kid? Maybe I could buy a cup of coffee with this cash."

What did he expect a ten-year-old kid to have? Whatever, Primo pocketed the money and discarded the wallet with the other items.

Collin had collected some of Nora's valuables: the sterling silver cutlery and tea set from the dining room, wedding gifts from years ago; her jewelry box containing several high-priced necklaces, bracelets, and earrings; her laptop; and an envelope with a couple hundred dollars of petty cash Dave kept in the nightstand by their bed. These items as well as a few others Primo picked up and put back in the plastic bag.

Then he looked at his two compatriots. "Hey, jerk-offs, gather up this loot and take it to the van. Grab all the televisions and computers in the place, too."

As Bareface and Dumbass collected the items, Primo looked over at Deet. "Get off your ass and strap this kid back up. Then take this chick around to do her duty. And keep your hands off her. At least for now, anyway. I'll see about later." He turned and pinched Sonya on the cheek before she jerked her head away, so forcefully her chair shook, then moved an inch across the carpet.

Deet quickly shot out of the chair and approached Collin, who was sitting quietly on his chair in the middle of the room. When Collin moved his own arms to the back, Deet bound his wrists and feet again. Deet's hands shook when he moved behind Sonya and cut the tape off her hands and feet. As soon as she was free, she leaped up and darted toward the stairs with the knife-wielding Deet rushing to catch up to her.

Again, footsteps resounded from the ceiling as Sonya and Deet traveled from bedroom to bedroom. When they descended the stairs, Deet dragged a bulky sheet wrapped around more of Nora's possessions into the living room. By the time these monsters were through with their wicked caper, nothing would remain. Hopefully, this family would still have their lives.

Deet dropped the sheet and its contents near the items Primo had discarded. Primo arose from the couch to check out the new bounty while Sonya and Deet left the living room to search the remainder of the house.

The newly added chattel didn't impress Primo much. He picked up Nora's fur coat, scrutinized it, then looked at her. "Old woman, is this thing worth anything?"

Nora stared at him. "I don't know. It was a gift from my husband. I never asked him how much it cost. That would have been rude."

In truth she knew exactly what it cost. She and Dave had gone shopping one Christmas and saw it on the rack in the department store. It looked and felt like a mink coat. Of course, it was a good synthetic imitation. She would never buy a real fur coat, knowing what those poor animals would have sacrificed for her vanity. But she wouldn't admit that to this creep. Let him think it was genuine. Let him try to pawn it or give it to some woman—then find out it was a fake. She snickered as he looked away and placed it in his *to keep* pile.

A couple of pairs of designer jeans Sonya had brought from home were in the sheet. Primo held them up, noticed the brand name, and threw them on top of the fur coat.

Then he picked up a small, black velvet box. It didn't look familiar to Nora. She assumed it was Sonya's. Primo opened it and took out a gold locket. "Hmm. This yours, old lady?"

Nora shook her head, wondering where Sonya had gotten it. It looked pricey. Maybe her father bought it for her. He was being more attentive to the kids lately.

As they discussed this unfamiliar item, Dumbass and Bareface returned from loading the van. Sonya and Deet came back carrying another sheet full of Nora's belongings. Sonya strutted to her chair and immediately dropped down, folding her arms in front of her. Dumbass approached her, grabbed her arms, twisting them behind her, and bound her again.

With Sonya seated, Primo, still holding the locket and little, velvet box, glanced over at her with that same shitty attitude. "Old woman, did you know this little bitch has a boyfriend?" He put his face close to Sonya's, but she turned her head sideways. She sat up straight, trying to ignore him, but he continued to harass her. "You go all the way with this dude yet, little chickie? Does your mama know? I bet you had *fun*. Maybe you and me can have some fun tonight too. What do ya say?"

Primo laughed as he replaced the locket into the box and slid it in his pocket.

Sonya's face was fiery red, and her tense body trembled. Nora wanted to comfort her, but she was helpless. Sonya turned toward Nora as her grandmother shook her head and mouthed *I'm sorry*. Sonya's expression changed from anger to sadness, her mouth turning down and her eyes filling with tears. She nodded her head at Nora as if to say *I understand.*

Primo found a few other things he placed in the pile he intended to keep. When he picked up a battered black case, Nora recognized it immediately. It came from Dave's office. Dave was a knife collector. He was not a violent man, but he appreciated the craftsmanship of good quality knives. That scruffy, black box contained a pair of knives from the seventeenth century used in a duel between two French painters over the love of the same damsel. The knives were priceless.

Dave always said, "I should keep these in a safe deposit box or in the office safe with my other knives instead of in my desk drawer. But I want them handy so I can enjoy them more often. I love to take them out of their case and caress the cold, sharp, metal blades and intricate handles while I imagine the tragic battle fought with them."

According to legend, it had been a bloody battle with both men being mortally wounded. The young damsel for whom the duel was fought was so distraught with the horrible deaths of both her lovers that she removed both knives from their bodies and simultaneously plunged them into her own heart.

Nora didn't want to part with those knives, not because of their value, but because they meant so much to Dave. It soon became evident by the manner in which Primo stared at them when he opened the case that he wanted them. His eyes stretched open beyond their normal expanse, and his arm jutted toward the ceiling. "My, my! What have we here?"

He removed them from the case and stroked them in a similar fashion as Dave had often done. To control her anger, Nora turned away from seeing the pleasure in his eyes and tried taking deep breaths, letting the air out slowly.

Neither Sonya nor Collin knew anything about the knives. Dave had chosen not to show them to the grandkids until they were older. Amy and Brian knew of their existence but also never spoke of them to their kids. Thus, when Sonya and Collin noticed Nora's discomfort, they had no idea what was wrong. Both of them gave her a puzzled look. Nora glanced at them and closed her eyes while shaking her head rapidly. She was damn sure she was not going to remotely indicate their financial or sentimental value to that monster.

While Primo admired the knives, he asked, "Where you get these, old woman? They worth some big bucks?"

Nora refused to look at him when she answered. "I have no idea. They belong to my husband."

"Hmm. I like these. I think I'll keep them." He laughed as he placed them on his pile. "You don't mind, do you, old hag?"

She looked down at the floor, trying to calm her emotions. What could she do?

Chapter Ten

Still Early Thursday Morning

Nora was still staring at her feet when Primo's boots appeared in her vision. He grabbed her chin and forced her to look up at him. "Okay, bitch. Your turn. And guess what. I'm gonna be your guide. Isn't that just what you been hopin' for? I bet you thought I had other plans, didn't you? You probably thought one of these two dimwits would trail your ass around, and you could get away with not givin' me that stack of money you have stashed somewhere. Sorry to disappoint you, old woman."

He turned to one of the other men. "Hey, Dumbass! Get over here and unbind this ole bag."

Dumbass quickly moved forward and cut the tape on Nora's arms and legs. No nicks to her skin. He was finally adept at cutting duct tape. She stood up, a little unsteady from arthritis and lack of circulation.

"What's the matter, bitch? This game too rough for an old hag like you?" Primo laughed and gave her a forceful shove. She staggered toward the stairs, catching her balance by grabbing the wall to avoid falling.

She didn't have a plan. She knew the kids had missed some things Primo would want, and she was torn whether or not she should reveal them. There was a chance those men would never find them if she didn't divulge their whereabouts. Then again, there was that chance they would. She knew this demon wasn't messing around when he said there'd be serious consequences if they didn't relinquish everything of value. After quick and rash thinking, she'd decide when she came to the items.

They first went into the bedroom used by Collin. Nothing worth much was in the bureau or dresser. It was evident that Collin had already examined them. Collin had also given these beasts anything of his own he thought was worth something, so Nora didn't bother checking his personal possessions. Poor kid. When he decided to stay with his grandmother, he never expected to have his privacy invaded like this.

She didn't store much of anything in this room's closet either. It had been a long time since Amy and Brian had moved away, and she and Dave didn't use their children's old bedrooms much. Possibly for the grandkids' visits or maybe occasional out of town guests. But she looked in the closet merely to be sure. Wrapping paper and gift boxes lined the shelf above the clothing bar. A few of her evening dresses covered in plastic garment bags hung on the bar. Even though they were expensive dresses, Primo had no use for them. Just to be sure, she wrapped her arm around a couple of them. "Do you want these?"

He glared at her. "Hell, woman. What you think I am? A homo?"

She left the dresses hanging in the closet, walked to the middle of the room, looked around for a few seconds, and then went out the door to Amy's old room where Sonya was staying. Anything of Amy's was removed years ago, and Sonya had picked through her own things already. The bureau in this room held extra bath towels and wash clothes used when they had guests. These items were dumped on the floor. The closet held extra blankets in case the winter nights were cold. The blankets were also scattered in the middle of the room. Thus, she found nothing in this room worth removing.

The connecting bathroom to these two bedrooms also was barren except for Collin and Sonya's personal toiletries. Nora briefly looked in the linen closet. Nothing worth taking. A few containers of extra shampoos, conditioners, lotions, and soaps were all in disarray. One of the bottles must've broken. A white creamy liquid had settled in a puddle under several containers, and a bottle of body lotion lay on its side in the middle of the gooey, opaque mess.

Next she went to the spare bedroom. Televisions had been in all the bedrooms. These thieves had already removed all of the electronics and taken them to their vehicle, which according to the police officer and Primo's earlier remark, was a van, definitely large enough to accommodate their ill-gotten gains taken from her house. Someone had removed the bedding and turned the mattress, apparently to look for money or other valuables underneath. They would've come away empty-handed.

Nora didn't recall ever keeping anything of value in this room's closet, but she checked just to be sure: Dave's tuxedo in another garment bag; some Halloween costumes he and Nora had worn to various parties over the years. Nothing else. She left that room to go to the hall bathroom.

She and Dave rarely used this bathroom, so it was fairly empty except for cleaning supplies and toilet paper. Nora looked in the medicine cabinet just to show Primo it was empty, and then backed out of the room to go to Dave and her bedroom.

She couldn't get used to calling it just *her* bedroom. Maybe if and when this ordeal ended. Maybe she shouldn't think of stupid things like that when her life and that of her grandchildren were at stake.

As she walked into their room, she thought of the iron pipe that should be under the bed and wondered if it was still there. She didn't want to take the chance of stooping over to check. Perhaps she missed it in the things Collin or Sonya brought downstairs. She was disappointed she couldn't check, for she had counted on somehow confiscating that pipe to use as a weapon against these beasts. Undoubtedly, she couldn't grab it while being watched by Primo, but she hoped an opportunity might eventually avail itself. With any luck, that might still be an option. She had to have hope.

The kids had retrieved everything they thought was of value to Primo from the master bedroom, including the jewelry Nora kept in her jewelry box. Her most expensive pieces were in the family safe. The family safe. Could she avoid opening it when she led Primo into Dave's office? There was that chance Primo wouldn't notice it behind a bronzed framed copy of the Ten Commandments in back of Dave's mahogany desk. Other framed documents and pictures lined the walls in the office. Maybe Primo would miss it. But did she want to take that chance and suffer the consequences if he discovered it? She would make that decision when they went downstairs.

She hadn't done anything with Dave's clothes in his closet yet. It was much too soon to think about disposing or donating them. As she riffled through his suits and shirts, tears came to her eyes. If he were with her today, these scoundrels wouldn't be taking advantage of an old woman and her young grandchildren. He would somehow put a stop to this madness before it went this far.

It was obvious the kids had already rummaged through the shelves above the clothes and the shoes below. She didn't remember anything unusual that Dave kept in the closet. She turned to Primo, who was standing directly behind her. "Do you want any of these suits or shirts? They're of very good quality. My husband dressed well." With her little finger, she wiped away a stray tear gathering at the corner of her eye.

He glared at her again; it seemed like he often brandished these looks. "What would I want with an old dead man's clothes? You think I need these?" He pushed her out of the closet, grabbed a handful of shirts, ripped them from their hangers, and tossed them on the floor. Then he grabbed her arm and pulled her away. "Quit sniveling. Get your ass out here and find me the good stuff."

She staggered to her own closet. Just clothes, shoes, and purses. Some of the purses were posh designer bags. She threw most of them out onto the bedroom floor. "These are worth money. They're originals." That was true about some of the handbags, but some of them were knock-offs. She had planned to get rid of several of them eventually. Thus, she didn't care if he took any of them.

He picked up a twelve-inch, beige leather handbag with the insignia of the designer pressed and engraved into the leather. He opened the clasp, looked inside, and stretched his left arm out with the opened bag dangling from his arm. "How much this one worth?"

"It's not new, so it has depreciated in value. You could probably get three or four hundred dollars for it," she lied. That particular bag was not an original. She had picked it up a few years ago at a discount women's clothing store and had planned to give it to charity.

Primo jerked upright. "You pay crazy money like that for a purse? What's the matter with you?"

"You're right. It's silly. But if I hadn't bought them, you wouldn't be able to steal them from me now, would you?" She picked up the handbags and put them in one of the pillowcases from the bed.

"Don't get smart with me, bitch!"

She chuckled under her breath.

Other than some of the handbags, Nora couldn't think of anything else of value in the bedroom. She walked into the master bath, leaving the purses on the floor.

The medicine cabinet still held all of Dave's prescription drugs for his heart condition. Her blood pressure, thyroid, and arthritis medications were also on those shelves. She opened the doors of the cabinet so Primo could see inside. "Do you want any of these medications?"

He seized a few, looked at their labels, and dropped those he looked at into the sink. He examined all of them. "Yeah, throw them in something. Good stuff here."

She retrieved a folded pillowcase from the linen

closet, placing all the vials of prescriptions into it.

Ah, the linen closet. It was next. On the middle shelf set the backup shampoos, conditioners, and lotions that she and her husband used. Something else, something very significant also rested among the toiletries. That something just might help her and the kids out of their horrible predicament. She had a gun hidden in a box of panty liners.

****

Maybe Dave had experienced some kind of premonition. A few years ago, he bought a gun. Since they lived in a rural, sparsely populated area of the county and with crime and violence increasing daily, he wanted it for protection. He purchased a Smith & Wesson two-inch J Frame .357 magnum revolver. Its barrel held five bullets. They practiced shooting it several times back in their woods. Where they would hide the gun was the topic of a long and quarrelsome discussion between them.

They both agreed the gun should be easily accessible. Dave made his first suggestion. "Let's store it in a locked gun box in the closet."

Nora countered, "Bad idea. I believe the closet would be one of the first places a home invader would look for any type of weapon. If the gun box is locked, we'd both have to constantly carry a key around our neck in order to access that gun in an emergency."

He finally agreed, "Yeah, I guess you have a point there." He then suggested, "I'll build a shelf under the couch in the living room and attach the gun to it."

She shook her head. "No, no. Can you imagine you or me quickly getting down on our knees and stretching under that couch to retrieve the gun? Maybe we'd be able to grasp it, but heavens, it'd take us both five minutes to finally get up off the damn floor! That intruder wouldn't help us up or stand by and watch us struggle to our feet to point the gun at him."

"You're right. Scratch that idea."

Then she suggested, "Maybe we can hide it in a plastic bag in the clothes hamper among the dirty laundry." She refuted her own idea. "No. That won't work either. I get in and out of that hamper too often, and I'd constantly be jostling that gun while moving the clothes around. If we kept it loaded, the chance would exist that it might accidently fire and shoot me while holding a pair of your dirty underwear."

He smirked. "Right again, dear. So what other suggestions do you have?"

When that idea was nixed, she proposed, "What do you think about hiding it in a cereal box? A gun would fit in one of those giant-size boxes."

"Nora, let me identify the flaws of that plan. Suppose the bad guys were hungry and chose the frosted flakes for a snack. Wouldn't they be surprised to bite into the barrel of a gun? Or what if the grandkids were here and helped themselves to a bowl of crispy rice? What if the gun fell out of the box, breaking the ceramic bowl and maybe even firing at them?"

Needless to say, that idea was also vetoed.

At last, Nora came up with the perfect hiding place. "I got it! Remember what the gun dealer told us when we purchased the gun?"

"I know he told us how much it cost and the damage it could do."

"He told us something else too. He said, 'Hide it in plain sight.' Remember?"

"Uh, yeah. I remember that. So what?"

"You know we older ladies sometimes deal with a little bit of a problem with bladder leakage. But at our age, we have so many other more serious health issues we often just deal with this minor issue. The way I deal with it is to use those thin panty liners on a regular basis."

He looked puzzled. "Nora, what does all this female talk have to do with hiding a gun? Do I really need to hear this?"

They were having this discussion in bed. She smiled and touched his hand. "Just listen. I'm getting to the point."

"Okay. I can't wait for the punchline."

She smiled and squeezed his hand. "I keep my current supply of liners that I use daily under the bathroom sink, right?"

"If you say so. Frankly, I never paid much attention to where you kept them. Believe it or not, babe, that doesn't seem too important to me."

She chuckled. "Well, I do, anyway. Whether you care or not. But the important thing is I like to have a spare box on hand too. I don't ever want to run out of this necessity."

"Okay, I guess I can agree with that. So?"

"So…in the linen closet with our backup supply of shampoo, toilet tissue, toothpaste, and other toiletries, I keep a new box of thin liners. What if we put the gun in this box? On the bottom of the box, I'll leave a few for cushioning purposes. On this cushion, I'll set the revolver. Atop the revolver, I'll place the rest of the liners to camouflage the gun. Voila! Problem solved. What thief would think to look in a box of lady's sanitary napkins? What do you think, dear?"

He squeezed her hand. "I think that's an ingenious idea, my love. That's where we'll hide it." They kissed, and their gun discussion ended while they engaged in more enjoyable activities.

****

While Nora surveyed the contents of the master bathroom linen closet—shampoos, lotions, cosmetics, towels—with Primo by her side, she glanced at the box of thin panty liners that concealed the revolver. It sat in plain view of both her and Primo. She pushed all the items around, pretending to look for something of value. Primo kept close watch as she rearranged the items. Finally, she moved away. "Nothing in here unless you think you could use a bottle of conditioner. Your hair is probably all matted down under that cap. It might need some extra care."

"Don't be a smartass, bitch." He dragged her out of the bathroom, pushing her into the bedroom. She had no opportunity to grab that revolver.

After she picked up the pillowcases from the bedroom, she walked into the hallway. He shoved her toward the staircase. She quickly clutched the railing to avoid toppling down the stairs and hurried ahead of him.

In the living room, Nora dropped the pillowcases on the floor. Then she went into the kitchen and gave it a cursory look. The kids had managed to get whatever these thieves wanted from this room. Dishes, food boxes, cutlery were scattered everywhere. The knife container on the counter was empty. Apparently, they had possession of all of those. Nothing left for her to confiscate in that room. Same thing in the dining room.

Collin had already retrieved Nora's sterling silverware set from the china cabinet. The family room and the sun porch had also been ransacked thoroughly.

Nora walked into the downstairs bathroom, opened the medicine cabinet and the linen closet, but knew no valuables were in that room.

Dave's office had to be next. She hadn't noticed the kids bringing anything from there into the living room except for his precious, antique knives. They probably assumed the room only held a bunch of paper files, office supplies, and books. Dumbass and Bareface had already removed the large desk computer, the laptop, and the printers. For the most part, the kids were correct. Why would these jerks be interested in copy paper, old bills and receipts, or even their prior years' tax returns? Apparently, they already knew Nora wasn't destitute or else they'd have targeted some other poor soul.

Like Amy had mentioned, scammers and thieves check the obituaries in local newspapers and online to find wealthy marks to rob. Nora didn't think she had put anything in Dave's obituary that would indicate her as an affluent widow. Perhaps the newspaper wasn't the culprit. After all, Sonya's friend, Deet, led these thugs to her house. She wondered what Sonya told Deet to make him believe she would be an easy pushover with lots of money and valuables. Sonya wouldn't intentionally have said anything to cause this havoc. Deet told Nora he'd explain why he led those jerks here, but did it really matter? They were in this predicament regardless of how they got there. She had to concentrate on getting them out of it.

As she stood momentarily in the middle of the

office, she needed to decide whether or not to fess up about the existence of the wall safe behind the framed Ten Commandments. Its content was of significant value. Probably about fifty or seventy-five thousand dollars in cash; stocks and bonds worth hundreds of thousands; the remainder of Dave's knife collection of undetermined value; and her best jewelry worth an additional several thousand. If they took off with all of those valuables, she'd be in some serious financial trouble. Should she take the chance Primo wouldn't look behind the Ten Commandments if she didn't bring the safe to his attention? He seemed like a seasoned criminal. As the expression goes—this wasn't Primo's first rodeo.

Much to her dismay, he made the decision for her. He grabbed her arm and firmly twisted it. "Okay, old woman, I know you're keeping something from me. I know you got more money in this house than you or those brats brought to me. Where is the safe? Is it in here, or were we already in the room where it's located, and you neglected to tell me? If that's the case, you are now in very serious shit."

With a tight grip on her arm, he gave her no choice. She had to reveal the safe's location. Looking down at her feet but pointing with her free arm to the framed Ten Commandments, she muttered, "It's behind that document." Then she faintly mumbled, "It would behoove you to read and obey those words in that frame."

"What'd you say, bitch?"

"Nothing. Nothing."

"Then get your ass over there and open that safe."

When he shoved her forward, her hip banged

against the desk. She squealed out in pain and limped around the desk. Slowly removing the Ten Commandments' large frame, she gently propped it against the shelving unit next to her. She stared at the safe for a couple of seconds, knowing the combination but stalling before entering it. But she knew it was inevitable.

"Get to it, woman; we ain't got all day."

She cleared her throat, rubbed her hands on her pant legs to absorb her sweaty palms, and then began.

With her hand shaking she slowly twisted the dial on the combination lock to the left four times past zero and then stopped at her first number, fifty. Next, she turned the dial to the right passing her second number, twenty-four, three times before stopping on it. Then she turned the dial left again passing her third number, thirty-five, twice before stopping on it. With the last step, she twisted the dial slowly to the right again approaching zero, waiting for the lock to click, signifying the safe was unlocked.

But Nora didn't hear the click. The safe didn't unlock.

Primo, who was breathing down her neck the entire time she attempted to unlock the safe, slapped her on the back of her head. "Woman! Quit stallin'. Get this damn safe open. Now!"

She rubbed the back of her head where he struck her. "I'm trying. I'm trying. But you're making me nervous standing on top of me like a vulture. Can't you back up a little and give me some space? You know I can't go anywhere, Primo."

Holy crap, she'd used his name. Hell! Now what could she do. More importantly, what would *he* do?

She didn't have to wait long to find out. He yanked her around so hard she thought he pulled her arm out of its socket. When he took her face in his hands like a vise, it felt like her jaw was breaking. Her ears reverberated when he yelled, "How come you know my name? Who told you my name, *bitch*?"

She didn't know what to say. Since she didn't know the circumstances regarding how Deet was involved in this crime spree, she didn't want to get him in deeper trouble than he already was. Her decision was to try to ignore his questions. Instead, she objected, "Stop! You're hurting me!"

But he didn't let up on his grip of her face. He stared at her with his eyes narrowed to barely slits and sending out spittle and bad breath from his mask. "How do you know my name, bitch?"

"I don't know! I don't know. I must've heard one of your henchmen call you that. I don't remember." She was scared out of her wits at that point. Would he believe her?

"Who? Who did it? Which one?"

She didn't think it was possible, but his grip got tighter on her jaw. She could barely open her mouth to talk. "I...I don't remember."

"You don't remember? *You don't remember?*" His voice got louder and more menacing.

Her voice came out in a squeak. "No."

Then he released her jaw and spun her around. Grabbing her by the arm and hair, he dragged her into the living room. She couldn't help herself. She cried out in pain, "Please stop!"

When they reached the living room, he threw her against the couch. The kids were screaming, seeing and hearing what was happening.

Primo turned to Sonya and Collin and slapped them hard in the face. The hit he gave Collin was so hard it knocked him and his chair onto the floor. He lay there struggling to upright himself.

Primo was a madman. To everyone's astonishment, he ripped off his mask and cap and threw them in Nora's face. She stared at him in wide-eyed disbelief. Did he figure he had nothing to gain by keeping them on any longer since she knew his name?

Despite terror enveloping her very being, she knew she'd never seen this man before. After he removed his cap, his sandy-colored hair sprouted like weeds from his scalp. His squared jawline, covered with a miniscule layer of hair, jutted prominently from his face. Like Bareface, this man was a stranger to Nora. A stranger who had come to destroy her and her grandchildren.

Primo's face was so red it looked like his head would explode in any second. Filled with fury and rage, his intense, marble eyes popped wide open. He breathed rapidly through his angled, pointed nose while he stomped around the room. He approached Dumbass and with both his hands grabbed him by the shirt, twisting it against his neck. "Did you tell this bitch my name?"

"No man, no! Why would I do that?"

Primo pushed Dumbass against the wall and plodded over to Bareface, who saw him coming and put his hands up in front of his chest, palms out. "Hey man, me neither. I didn't do it. You outta know that."

Primo was seething while staring at Bareface, who was visibly shaking and trying to back away from him. But Primo also caught him by the shirt and pulled Bareface toward him until their noses were almost touching. "You sure you didn't tell this bitch my name? Maybe you told that chick and she told the bitch. That the way it was?"

"No man. Honest. I never said nuthin about you. Never! Come on!"

Primo released Bareface. Still breathing heavily, Primo looked around the room. His eyes focused on Deet, who sat on a chair in the corner looking down at his feet with his arms crossed and his elbows on his knees. It was difficult to tell if he was crying or merely so scared his body was trembling. Primo slowly walked over to him. He stood in front of him for a few seconds before speaking. Then he growled, "Stand up, weasel."

Deet cautiously arose from the chair, still looking at the floor.

"Look at me, asshole!"

Deet raised his eyes to look at Primo's face. In one swift motion, Primo clutched his left ear, twisting it tightly in his hand. Deet cried out in pain, his knees collapsing, but Primo lifted him back up off his feet and threw him into the chair. "You did this! Didn't you?"

Deet's face was riddled with a look of terror. He croaked, "Uh, it was an accident, man. It just slipped out. I didn't mean it, Primo. I didn't mean it. Honest. I didn't mean it."

Nora, on the couch and still in pain from the abuse Primo had awarded her in the office, felt terrible about being the reason Deet was getting the brunt of Primo's wrath. She hadn't meant for this to happen. But hell, being in her predicament, anything was possible. Regardless, she had to try to help the situation. "He didn't mean to tell me your name. It truly was a slip of the tongue. Don't hurt him."

Primo turned to look at her. His arm swiftly jerked forward and pointed. "Shut your friggin' mouth, bitch!"

She should've realized whatever she said wouldn't make any difference to him. He was beyond rational thinking. He turned back to Deet. "You really messed things up."

"I'm sorry, Pr...I mean, dude. It won't happen again."

Primo gripped a handful of Deet's hair. "You're right, you bastard. It won't. Because you're gonna join these friggin' buttheads."

Primo literally lifted Deet off the chair and tossed him onto the couch next to Nora. The man had unbelievable strength. As Deet landed, his left hand unintentionally swung out and hit Nora hard in her right eye. She shrieked and put both her hands on it. Her eye felt like it had been knocked to the back of her skull. As she moaned from the pain with both her eyes closed, she experienced an unexpected hard slap to her face, causing her to roll against Deet. Primo roared, "Bitch, you better shut up before I kill you."

Nora had about all she could take. She knew she was being foolish, but her emotions took over again, dulling her sense of duty to her grandchildren and numbing any desire to cooperate with this madman. She shouted at him with one hand still over her right eye, "Go ahead. Kill me, you monster! See how much money you get then!"

Simultaneously, Sonya and Collin, who had somehow managed to upright himself and his chair, cried out in response to Nora's words, "No Granny, no!" Sonya also screamed, "Please don't make him madder. Please!"

109

Then there were four captives crying and sobbing—Sonya, Collin, Nora, and Deet. Nora didn't say another word. They were all waiting to see what Primo would do next. He was pacing the room, getting angrier by the second. Then he stopped in front of Dumbass, and much to everyone's surprise, he ripped off Dumbass' mask and cap, hurling them to the floor. Dumbass threw his hands to his face. "Hey, man, whatchu do that for?" He rubbed his face where the ripping off of the mask had stung him.

Primo pulled back and thrust his right arm out in the direction of Dumbass. His anger was still very evident, as they heard every heavy breath he took when he spoke. "Let me introduce you to my friend and colleague, Tonto Ramirez. Say hello to these fine folks, Tonto." He stood back, gawking at Dumbass and waiting for his response.

Dumbass looked pleadingly at Primo. "Man, why you doin' this? I didn't do nuthin' wrong."

But Primo continued his ranting. "We are one happy family now, aren't we? By the way, Tonto here is the esteemed uncle of that little weasel, Deet. Of course, Tonto isn't your real name is it, Tomas?" Primo glared at Dumbass again. "Tell these fine people why even your mama and papa don't call you by Tomas."

Sheepishly Tonto, aka Dumbass continued to plead, "Cut it out, dude. Whatchu tryin' to do, man?"

"Well," gloated Primo, "they call him Tonto because in Spanish it means a very stupid person. Ain't that right, Tonto?" Primo paused, but there was no response from anyone. He wasn't done with Tonto yet. "Yeah, stupid dumb. Ha!" He let out a hysterical laugh. "He's not the sharpest tool in the shed. What a pair, right? An airhead and a wimpy rat fink."

Bareface tried to reason with Primo. "What are you doin', man? This ain't necessary. Let's get on with our business."

Primo stopped taunting Tonto and looked viciously at Bareface. He slowly sauntered over to him. "Now, folks, this here fine gent is my bestie bud. Right, Nails? My bestie bud, indeed! Mister Bobby Naylor, folks." Primo put his arm out toward Nails, formerly known as Bareface."

Shaking his head, Nails looked disgustedly at Primo.

Primo grinned dementedly and began to wobble his head. "Now, now, Nails, my boy. We must make these folks feel comfy in their own home. Right?" He walked over to the side of the couch where he faced the constrained quartet. And he bowed, tucking his left arm behind his back and extending his right arm toward the foursome, still with the gun in his hand. "And I, my good friends, am Alan Priestley." More deranged laughter. "Thanks to that weasel over there, you know me as Primo, your boss man. Your head honcho. Your top gun. Don't cha think I have a perfect name? Ain't I so priestly?" He snickered, his eyes wide and disturbed.

The captives now not only saw their captors' faces but they knew them by their real names. And Primo had become more of a madman.

Chapter Eleven

Nigh on to Thursday's Dawn

Nora figured she'd refer to these bastards by the same names they called each other. Tonto, Nails, and Primo. Why not? They were all just one happy family now. Seemed like no matter what she did, she couldn't change whatever plans Primo had for them. With the faces and the real identities these vile fiends revealed, Nora and the kids were doomed. She had to come up with something. God help them!

After Primo's rampage settled, he went to one of the empty chairs and slumped into it. His eyes roamed the room, focusing on everyone, even his cronies. No one uttered a word. They waited. After about ten minutes of silence, Tonto was the first to chance speaking. "Hey, uh, Primo. Okay if I calls you Primo? Everybody knows your name now." He paused. "Uh, you want I should tape up li'l Deet and the old lady?"

Primo stared at Tonto for a few seconds. "Yeah, you do that, stupid." He remained seated while looking around the room. Perhaps he was trying to figure out what *his* next action should be.

Suddenly, Primo stood up. "Hold on there, Tonto. Just tape up the little weasel. That bitch has a job to do." He walked toward Nora. "Stand up, you old hag. You still need to open that safe."

Nora hadn't forgotten about the safe. She had hoped Primo didn't remember. Who was she kidding? She knew for damn sure he would never forget. Why else were these monsters here? Not just for the things they already collected from the house. No. They wanted the big money. They wanted everything of value that she possessed. Otherwise, they would've been long gone. But no matter how much money, how many televisions and other electronics they stole from her, she had to protect what was most important, Sonya and Collin. And the fact that she couldn't open the safe made the possibility of keeping them out of danger very unlikely. She feared their real torture was just beginning.

She stood up immediately and walked toward Dave's office. Primo followed close behind with the gun at her back. When they entered the room, she asserted, "If you stand so close to me breathing down my neck, the same thing will happen as last time. I'll be too nervous to correctly enter the combination."

He gave her a snarly look, pushed her deeper into the room, but remained near the desk as she staggered to the safe. She took a deep breath and silently prayed she wouldn't be too tense this time. She had no choice. She had to give him the contents of the safe. She could think of no way to get around it. After a second deep breath, she wiped her sweaty hands again on her pants, and started her daunting task.

Flexing and steadying her fingers, she began. Left four times past zero; stop at fifty; right three times; stop at twenty-four; left two times, stop at thirty-five; right until it clicked. But it didn't click!

She was so confused. She didn't understand, for

she was certain she used the correct combination. She had opened the safe a few times before without difficulty, so she knew how to do it. Why wouldn't it open this time? Surely if Dave changed the combination, he would've given her the new one. She didn't know what to do. One thing for certain—she really was riddled with fear now. "I don't understand." She turned to face Primo. "I put in the correct combination. It should've opened."

Primo glared at her so intensely she thought he might shoot her at that very moment. "Quit messing with me. Open that friggin' safe, Now!"

Nora vigorously shook her head. "I'll try again, but I know that was the combination, and I did it right. I don't understand. My husband must've changed the combination on me. Really, I know I have to give you what's in the safe, but I just can't open it." She begged, "Please, believe me!"

Primo slapped her on her left cheek and then her right. "Open that damn safe, bitch! I'm tired of your friggin' games."

Screaming, she protested, "It's not a game. I can't open it! The combination won't work. He must've changed it. I'm sorry. I'm sorry."

Primo didn't accept her meager apology. He grabbed her arm so tightly it felt as if he held onto the bone itself. He dragged her out from behind the desk. When he brutally shoved her forward, she fell to her hands and knees. He kicked her. "Get up!"

She quickly crawled to the chair in front of Dave's desk and pulled herself up. As soon as she was standing, he shoved her again, but this time she stayed upright. She stumbled back to the living room. He pushed her onto the couch again and moved to the middle of the room. "Nails, bind that bitch back up. Tonto, cut that boy loose."

Nails took Nora's arm, dragged her to the vacant dining room chair, and began to bind her hands behind her back. Tonto started removing the tape from Collin's wrists. Colin's face turned white. Quickly, Nora protested, "What are you going to do with him?"

Once more Primo gave her his evil stare. "Since you refuse to cooperate and open the safe, maybe you need a little persuasion."

"I'm not refusing. I'd open it if I could." She was so hysterical her voice didn't even sound like it came from her.

"Okay. Since you *didn't* open the safe, somebody must be punished. And I pick that little squirt."

"What are you going to do to him?"

"I'm just gonna do to him whatever it takes for you to open that safe?"

"*No!* I told you I can't open it. Wait! Do something to me, not him. He's just a kid."

"Do you think I don't know that? Why do you think I picked him? And if after I'm done with him, you still don't open that safe, I'm gonna take that pretty little girlie over there. Oh, what me and my boys can do to her! I might even let Deet join in." Primo gave Deet a sly glance. "Wouldn't you like that, Deet, ole boy?"

Nora couldn't let any of that happen, but she couldn't think straight. Her mind raced to come up with some alternative while she focused on Primo's words. "No! Wait! Maybe we can handle it some other way."

"Old woman, if you think these studs would rather climb on top of your wrinkled ass instead of that sweet little juicy plum, you got a few screws loose in that head of yours."

His idea was revolting and far from what Nora had in mind. She was disgusted to even think about that possibility. God forbid. If she could oblige them in that manner to keep these kids safe, she'd do it in a heartbeat. But no chance of that happening. Like the monster said, these virile men thought of her as repulsive as she thought of them.

Quickly, she came up with another possibility. "No, I don't mean that. I mean, since I can't open the safe, what if I go to the bank and get you the money I have there? I could do that as soon as the bank opens. Then you would leave us alone, right?" She was rambling, trying to think of something, anything to appease this devil.

The men took the bait. Everybody stopped. Nails halted binding Nora's arms. Tonto stopped cutting the tape on Collin's wrists. Everyone waited for Primo's reaction to her wild suggestion.

Primo slightly lifted his head. He puckered his lips, and his eyes were darting back and forth. Was he considering her reckless proposal? He went to the couch and sat directly in front of her. "How much can you get me at the bank?"

Since she had pulled that idea out of a hat, Nora hadn't the foggiest idea how much money was in their joint savings account. She usually only accessed the checking account, which was sufficient for any spending she did. Dave always handled deposits and withdrawals from the savings and kept an ample balance in the checking for household needs. Besides, if she wanted to withdraw a very large sum of money, how would she even do it?

"Uh, I'm not exactly sure, but I know there's a couple hundred thousand there. I don't know how to get it out, but I can find out. How would that work? I'd get you that money, and then you'd leave, right?" More rambling and wishful thinking.

Nora waited while Primo tossed the proposition in his mind. Even though it was a "Hail Mary" attempt on her part to save their asses, there was that slight chance it might resonate with Primo. She doubted if he had expected her to say that much money was in the account, which made the idea more appealing to him. But she knew for certain, if she wanted him to take her seriously, she had to offer him enough of an incentive. She'd give anything to get him out of her house and out of their lives forever.

Primo sat back on the couch. "Tonto, leave the kid alone for now. Nails, finish binding up that bitch. Me? I got to think about this."

At least he was considering the idea. Nora tried to encourage his thoughts in the right direction. "As soon as the bank opens, I'll go in and request my money. I've never withdrawn that much before, so I don't know what I'll have to do. But surely we can work this out. Maybe I should call them first to find out how to access the money."

He stared at her. "How do you find out how much money you got in that bank? Don't they send you something to let you know? Don't you keep track of what you got?"

"My husband always handled our finances. He was better at it than I. But I know where the bank paperwork is located. I can check our last statements."

When Nails finished binding Nora's hands, Primo interrupted. "Hold up on the rest of the tape." He focused on Nora again. "Okay woman, you get those statements, and let's look at them. Maybe we can make a deal after all."

After Nails sliced the tape around her wrists, she stood. "They're in the office."

Primo also stood. "Okay, bitch, let's go."

She hurried to the office and went directly to the filing cabinet next to the back window. Dave had kept all their financial information in that cabinet: bank statements, broker statements, tax returns. The stocks and bonds themselves were in the safe. She located the files for the checking and savings accounts and pulled out April's statements, carrying them over to the desk. Primo followed right behind her. She first looked at the checking account statement. "There's $21,394.76 in this account." She placed it aside and checked the balance on the savings account. "On this account, there's $388,776.83."

"Hot damn, woman, now we're talkin'! You got real bucks to give me."

She simply shook her head.

"Okay. Grab those papers, and we're gonna discuss this." He dragged her back into the living room. "Sit on the couch." Holding the statements and holding out for hope, she obeyed. He pulled one of the side chairs closer to the couch. "Lemme see those papers."

She thrust them toward him, and he looked over them for several minutes. Then he waved them in the air. "Look, guys, we're gonna be rich."

Both Tonto and Nails came over to see the bank statements. Nails grabbed the savings. "Shit, man.

That's a lotta dough. We can get this?"

"This bitch says we can. We're gonna test her, and if she doesn't, then she might as well kiss those little kiddies goodbye."

Since Nora didn't know if there was a chance in hell she could pull this off, she remained silent. But she sure as hell wasn't going to tell those assholes of her uncertainty.

Tonto gawked at the savings statement. "Wow! We gonna be rich!"

Nora looked out the window into the front yard. The sun was beginning to break through the trees, and its early rays glistened off the vivid butterflies on her metal sculpture in her garden. It was going to be light soon, and decisions and plans had to be made.

Primo laid the bank statements on a side table and got out of the chair. "I'm gonna take a nap. Tape this woman back up and keep your eyes on them. Wake me at eight o'clock. We need to get to the bank."

He went upstairs.

Chapter Twelve

Thursday Morning

Heads bobbing and shoulders slumping in discomfort, the four prisoners dozed in their chairs for the next couple of hours. Nails and Tonto sat on the couch to stand watch. Occasionally, Nora raised her head to see the men also with their eyes closed. However, she couldn't take advantage of their inattention because she and the kids were securely bound to their chairs.

She worked at the tape, trying to loosen it. It felt a little less tight but not enough to pull out her hands or feet. They were stuck in captivity and couldn't break loose. Even if they could, these guys had guns and knives, and they were big, adult men. What could the four of them do? An old woman and three kids? Actually, she wasn't sure about Deet. Yes, they tied him up, but was his allegiance still to his uncle? Could she count on his help if needed?

She was also worried about the money situation. Would the bank simply let her withdraw it? Even if it was her own money, how much does the bank have on hand that they'd be able to release several hundred thousands of dollars? The first thing she would do was to call the bank and get some answers. At least then she'd know what to expect before going there.

If only she could've opened that damn safe, all this would be over with, and these bastards would be gone. *Dave, why? Why did you change the combination to the safe? I know you never would've dreamed we'd be in this predicament, but why? Oh, Dave!*

While she was deep in thought, Sonya whispered, "Granny, are you gonna be able to get that money out of the bank?"

She didn't want to lie to Sonya. "I'm not sure, honey, but I'm sure as hell going to try. The thing is, even if I can't, it'll bide us a little more time."

Sonya gave her a sad, defeated look. "Yeah, I guess, but then what?"

She had to get Sonya to believe they'd put an end to this horrid situation even if she didn't have a clue at that time how it could be done. She had to give Sonya some hope.

Leaning toward her granddaughter, she mumbled, "Listen. We're going to get out of here one way or another. I've got some other ideas up my sleeve. Don't you worry. If I can't get the money from the bank, I'll come up with something else. Don't give up on us, honey. Please."

Collin had heard most of their whispering. He leaned toward Nora. "Granny, I know you. You're smart. You used to be a teacher. I know you'll get us out of this somehow. You're smarter than all those jerks put together."

She smiled at him while blinking back the tears forming in her eyes. "Thanks, Collin. I love you."

Collin was about to say something else when they heard someone's phone alarm go off. Nails jerked alert and looked at his smartphone on the side table. "Hey,

Tonto, wake up. Go get Primo. It's eight o'clock."
Nails got off the couch and began to walk around the
room, stretching his arms and loosening up his joints.
Tonto went upstairs to wake up his majesty.

The kids started shaking their heads, moving their
shoulders, and squeezing their eyes open and shut.
Those were the only movements possible to try to
improve circulation. They were as cramped as Nora
was from being in the same position for hours. This
crap had to end.

Physically, she felt wretched. Her eye throbbed and
watered. Her head ached from Primo's abuse. Her side
hurt from where he kicked her. She was a mess, but she
couldn't let the kids know how she felt. She knew they
were miserable too. And she needed to pee.

While waiting for the supreme master to come
downstairs, she looked out the living room window
again. Was that her red cardinal in the oak tree? Maybe
that's a good sign. Maybe Dave was sending her a
message. Perhaps things will be okay as soon as she got
these creeps her money. Maybe.

As she was grimacing from all her injuries, Sonya
looked at her and whispered, "Are you sure you're
okay, Granny?"

"Yes, honey," she said softly. "Just a few aches
and pains, but I'm all right. How about you?"

"Yeah, I'm okay. Uh, what's your plan for this
morning?"

"First thing, I have to call the bank to find out the
procedure. Then, I don't know. It depends on how these
monsters want to handle things."

Collin leaned toward her and murmured, "Granny,
do you think they'll let us go after they get the money?

After all, we saw their faces, and we know their names. That's pretty scary."

"Yeah, it is, son. I don't know what they plan to do with us, but as God is my witness, we're going to get out of this alive. Somehow." And she meant it too. That red cardinal was a sign. He had come back to give her strength. To help them find a way.

She thought of the revolver in the panty liner box upstairs in the bathroom linen closet. She had to get her hands on it. And the iron pipe was somewhere, maybe still under the bed.

Just as she was thinking about the pipe, Collin leaned toward her as close as he could. "Granny, when I was in your bedroom, I saw some big pipe sticking out from under the bed. I kicked it farther under a little bit before Tonto had a chance to see it. Did you know it was under there?"

"Oh, Collin, yes I did. I'm so glad you took the initiative to kick it out of sight. I wondered what happened to it. Since Primo was breathing down my neck in the bedroom, I didn't get a chance to reach for it. We'll find some way to get it."

When they heard Primo and Tonto coming down the steps, they stopped whispering. Nails met the other men in the hall, and they were discussing something the others couldn't hear. The three came into the living room. Primo ordered, "We gentlemen are hungry, woman. I'm gonna release you and the girlie so you can fix us some food."

"I don't have a lot of food in the house. My daughter is supposed to come tomorrow to bring us some groceries. I have eggs and maybe some frozen sausages. That'll have to do."

"Okay. Get to it."

Nails and Tonto removed the tape from Sonya and Nora, then sent them to the kitchen to prepare breakfast. Nails followed, evidently to thwart any escape attempt or weird activity they might try.

Sonya and Nora fixed the food. Nora had fourteen eggs and a package of frozen sausages. She fried all of it. Sonya thawed a loaf of bread from the freezer and toasted it. They served the food on paper plates and plastic cutlery. Primo was so kind as to let the captives eat what the three men didn't finish. The females ate first, making sure enough remained for the boys. Sonya and Nora were permitted to use the bathrooms with a guard posted at the door of each one. Then the men bound Sonya and Nora again, and Collin and Deet were released to eat. Before they were taped back up, the boys cleaned up the kitchen and were also allowed to use the bathrooms.

Primo sat in the middle of the couch in front of the four captives. "Okay, woman. What's your plan? How you gonna get my money?"

Even though she felt like saying some smartass remark about the mention of *his money*, she refrained. Instead, she suggested, "Before we go to the bank, I should first call to see how to withdraw the money and how much I can withdraw. I've never done anything like this before, and I don't know the protocol."

Surprisingly, Primo agreed, and her hands were undone. He handed her the bank statements so she could get the telephone number and account information. She took her phone from her pajama pocket and dialed the bank. It rang several times before it was answered.

"Hello, this is Nora Mitchell. My husband and I have our savings and checking accounts with you. I'd like to make a large withdrawal and was wondering what the procedure is."

She listened to the response, trying not to show any emotion. After they completed their explanation, she acknowledged, "Oh, I see. Well, all right. I'll probably be in this morning to fill out the form. Thank you for your information."

She hung up, sighed, and warily addressed Primo. "Well, this isn't going to be as easy as I thought."

He growled, "What do you mean?"

Before she could answer, her phone, still in her hand, rang. She looked at the screen. It was Amy. Believe it or not, she had completely forgotten about her. Amy often called her in the morning from her office. "I need to answer this. It's my daughter. If I don't, she'll be out here within the hour."

Primo tightly clasp her wrist. "You be careful what you say, bitch. Those kids' lives depend on it.

She knew she had to be calm and act as if three madmen were not in her house threatening to kill her and her grandchildren. She tapped the phone and answered Amy's call. "Hi, dear, are you at work yet?'

"Yes, I have so much to do. Dr. Petrakis is having a tax audit next week, and I'm not ready for it yet."

Nora had to calm her nerves. "Oh, that's too bad. Is anyone helping you prepare for it?"

"Oh, yeah. Josie is a big help, but there's so much that only I can do. Anyhow, Mom, is everything going all right? No more weird things happening?"

Nora tried to keep her voice from trembling as she reassured her daughter. "Oh, everything is fine. The kids are still sleeping. We plan to do some more fishing today. Maybe we'll get in a swim, too."

"That's good. I knew they'd be fine spending time with you. They have so much more to do out there than in the city. I'm glad you agreed to have them stay."

"Yes. We're having a great time." If only Nora could've thought of something to say to make Amy aware of the danger they were in, but with Primo staring at her, she couldn't think straight or fast enough.

"Well, okay, Mom. I'll be out tomorrow night to spend the weekend. Anything special you want me to get at the store before I come?"

"No, I can't think of anything. I'll ask the kids when they get up. See you tomorrow. Love you, Amy."

"Love you too, Mom."

Nora hung up. Amy didn't seem to suspect anything. Her voice sounded normal. She was worried about the tax audit at her office, so perhaps she didn't notice that Nora's voice sounded stressed and a bit shaky.

She put her phone back into her pocket and turned to Primo. "Okay, we have a couple of problems."

Primo spat out his question. "What do you mean we have problems? We have no problems. If we do, you'd better fix them or say goodbye to those kiddoes."

How was this going to work? To find out, she had to take a chance. "First of all, the bank. I'm allowed to withdraw as much of my money as I want."

He smiled that same wicked smile.

"However, I have to fill out a form and tell them how I plan to use the money. Per the government, any withdrawal of ten thousand or more must be documented. That's not the problem. I can make up some reason for needing the money. The problem is, it'll take four to seven business days for the bank to get that much money to my branch. They don't keep huge piles of cash on ha—"

Before she could finish her sentence, Primo exploded. He jumped off the couch and flailed his arms. "Shit! Shit! Shit!"

Even his two cronies looked wary. Sonya and Collin were terrified and ducked as far down as possible in their chairs. Nora had to somehow calm Primo down. "I know it doesn't sound good, but we can work around this. Okay?"

He stared at her with his fierce eyes burrowing into her. He pounded the side table, causing the lamp to tumble to the floor. "And how the hell can *we* work this out, bitch?"

"The bank person suggested I wire the money to your bank account. I'm sure I'd have to verify my identity, but it could all be done today. And you would have your money."

He snarled and glared at her as if horns were emerging from the top of her head. His demonic laugh exploded from his mouth. "Sure, sure, we can do that." He looked toward Nails and Tonto. "Great idea. Right, guys?" He turned back to Nora. "Except I don't have a bank account, smartass!"

"Shit!" she mumbled. "Then I don't know." She was at a loss. This was definitely not going well.

Primo sat down on the chair and closed his eyes, breathing so heavily it sounded as if he were about to take flight. Too bad that wasn't possible. No one said a word or made any kind of movements or sounds. Everyone waited for his next outburst.

It didn't take long. He burst out of the chair. "I need a drink." He marched out of the room.

Apparently, Primo had noticed Dave's bar in the office. He must've glanced over at it while Nora was trying to open the safe. Dave's liquor cabinet was well-stocked, and the small fridge held a few bottles of beer. Primo came back into the living room with an unopened bottle of Jim Beam. "Hey Nails, fix us some whiskey on the rocks. You guys up for it?"

With a gleam in his eye, Tonto grinned. "Yeah, man. Sweet!"

Nails took the bottle into the kitchen. Nora heard him getting into the freezer and clinking the ice cubes into the glasses. Soon he was back carrying the three drinks on a plate. He gave Primo his glass first, placed Tonto's on the table near him, and stopped in the middle of the room to take a swig of his own while placing the empty plate on a nearby table. "Damn! This stuff is friggin' good!"

The three of them continued drinking their whiskey. No one spoke. Nora was getting extremely worried. If these guys were ruthless when they were sober, how would they act when they got drunk? She also saw the concern on Sonya and Collin's faces. They were no strangers to drunken men. Amy had told Nora of the many times Carlos would come home drunk and mean, often frightening the kids so much they'd hide in their bedroom closets. Nora never asked Amy, but she assumed Carlos' drinking may have been a factor in their divorce.

When Primo had emptied his glass, he raised it up. "I need another one, Nails."

Nails put the empty glasses back on the plate and

took them into the kitchen, refilling them with a second round. When he returned with these, the three of them drank them a little more slowly.

This was not good. Things were bad enough before these bastards decided to start drinking. Who knew what would happen now? They were unpredictable when they were sober. Nora did know she had to get Primo back on track. They had to find a solution to the money issue. She wasn't sure how Primo would react with him being a little tipsy, but she had to take the chance and talk to him before he was too drunk for any reasoning.

She took a deep breath and mustered up her courage. "Uh, Primo, can we talk? Believe me. I want to solve this problem more than you do. Uh, maybe I can go to the bank today. One of you can go with me while the other two guard the kids. You know, if somebody is watching me, I won't do anything foolish that would jeopardize my grandchildren's safety. I can get all the paperwork handled today, and then we can wait out the days until the money arrives at the bank. I can make it clear to them that I'm in a hurry. Maybe that'll help the transaction go faster. Maybe I can convince them to have it ready by tomorrow afternoon. I could tell them it's an emergency."

The last thing in the world she wanted to do was spend who knows how many days with these madmen. Because of what the bank personnel told her on the phone, she realized there was very little hope of getting the money processed by the next afternoon, but what choice did she have? She had to convince Primo she could get it by then in order to at least provide her time to come up with something else. Sadly, she saw no other alternative that morning.

She knew the kids couldn't endure this mistreatment not knowing when or how it would end. Was she putting them too much at risk for Primo's complete meltdown when he finds out the money won't be available that soon? *Damn you, Dave!* If she had only opened that safe, these savages would be gone by now. Maybe.

She did get Primo's attention, but she wasn't sure if he was on board with the plan. His eyes looked glassy and unfocused. If she waited any longer, she knew he'd be too drunk to be remotely rational. She continued with her plan that she made up as she spoke. "Of course, I'd have to get more food. There isn't much in the house, but one of you can accompany me to the supermarket, too. Then you know I won't try anything sneaky because of the kids." She paused as he stared at her. "What do you say, Primo? Is it a deal?"

He didn't address her, but he turned to his buddy, Nails. "You think that's a good plan, dude? You think we can trust her? You think we can trust those kiddies?"

Nails, also fuzzy-eyed, slurred his words. "Hey, man, what choice do we have? That's a lotta green. We wouldn't have to pull any more jobs for a long time. We could take a long vacation. How about that?"

"Yeah, it is a lotta dough, but that's at least another day bein' cooped up in this crib with these friggin' imbeciles. Can we handle that?"

Tonto interrupted, "I can handle it. It's not so bad."

"Who asked you, dumbass?" growled Primo.

"Well, I'm okay with it," Tonto meekly offered.

Everyone was silent, waiting for Primo to make his

decision. It didn't matter that the other two bastards were okay with her plan. Primo had to be on board.

Finally, he sat up straight in his chair and clarified, "Yeah, I say that's our plan. Now woman, how we gonna make this work? You got to be real sure you can do this. Because if you don't... well, you know what'll happen."

Yes, Nora was well aware of the consequences. She had to be perfect in carrying out the plan. No mistakes. No tipping her hand in any way to anyone. She had to do it right. If not, the cost would be too catastrophic.

Again, she began to make up the plan as she spoke. "All right, I'm going to get dressed in a suit. I'll need to look proper. As for who goes with me, I think they should pretend they're another customer. Maybe enter the bank a few seconds behind me. I don't think your present apparel will work too well. Somebody dressed all in black might look suspicious. Whoever goes with me shouldn't look like a hoodlum, even though he is one. My husb—"

He cut her off. "Listen, bitch, I don't need no friggin' smartass comments. Get on with your idea."

She knew she should watch her tongue, although she glared at him. "Well, anyhow, whoever goes with me should change into an outfit from my husband's wardrobe so he'll look more presentable." She paused and looked at Primo. "Is that a better way to phrase it?"

He snorted. "Just get on with it, bitch."

"Okay. Whoever is my bodyguard should perhaps go over to one of the customer kiosks in the lobby and pretend he is filling out paperwork. He can still keep his eyes on me from that vantage point. I'll go to one of the tellers and ask to withdraw the money."

She hesitated.

"Go on, bitch. What's the matter?"

She took a deep breath. "Well, here might be the part where you may have to trust me."

Everyone stared at her with no idea what she planned to say.

"I truly don't know if the teller will simply hand me the form to fill out, or if I'll have to go in an office with another bank employee. I just don't know. But you know I'm concerned only for the safety of my grandchildren, so I would in no way jeopardize them. If I have to be away from my bodyguard's vision, I'll do nothing to cause harm to those children."

She stopped to wait for any reaction, but there was none. She continued, "After I fill out the paperwork, I should have a better idea when the money would be available. Then I'll give them the form and walk out of the bank with my bodyguard closely following behind. I'll park in the back parking lot so no bank personnel will see we are riding together in one car."

She stopped again. "I have a question."

She waited to see if Primo had any response. He didn't. She further explained, "As you know, there is over $388,000 in the savings account. If I thought it wouldn't matter, I'd give you every cent of it. But aside from getting you the money, the object here is not to raise any red flags or focus suspicion on what I'll be taking out of my accounts. Therefore, I think I should withdraw an even $300,000. That's a nice round figure. I plan to claim I'll be using it to purchase a piece of property in some foreign country like Costa Rica or Brazil, where foreigners can only purchase property with cash. That seems to be a believable lie. It's also a decent sum of money for the three of you to split, however you plan to do that.

She finished babbling. "What do you think? Does that sound okay to you?"

Nails pointed out, "That's a lotta money, dude. I'd be happy with my share. I agree with the old broad. We don't want to press our luck. We didn't expect to get away with even half that much. Let's go with her plan."

Primo was sobering up a bit. Nora was glad she had approached the problem when she did. He nodded his head. "Okay, old woman, we'll go along with most of your ideas, but I don't like the part of you goin' in some room without one of my boys. So we're gonna change it up a little bit. My man Nails is gonna be your lovin' nephew who looks out for his sweet old auntie. He goes where you go. Got that?"

She didn't like that scenario. No way would she attempt to relay to any bank employee about being held hostage, but she wasn't sure Nails as her nephew was going to seem credible. She had no choice but to go with it and hope for the best.

Maybe Primo was reading her thoughts. He threatened, "If you try to contact anyone while at that bank, these kiddies will be dead before you even get out of that bank door. And we'll be long gone."

She shuddered from his warning. "I promise I won't do anything to put these kids in any more danger."

"One more thing—yeah, three hundred grand is a lotta cash, but three hundred and fifty grand is better soundin' to me. This way you keep enough change to still look good."

He waited for her reaction. She had none. Then he threw his right arm forward. "Bitch, get your ass ready to go to the bank."

There was something else they had to discuss. Amy planned to spend the coming weekend with her and the kids. "Uh, there's one more thing."

"What the hell is it now?"

"My daughter intends to come and stay the weekend with us. She was coming tomorrow evening and bringing us groceries. I'm worried that she might arrive before you men have vacated my house. I don't want to endanger her life too. So I'll need to convince her not to come. I'll call her when she gets home from work tonight. Otherwise, she'd be leaving directly from work tomorrow afternoon."

"Damn, old woman, you sure can piss me off."

Nails unbound Nora's feet and followed her upstairs to wait while she changed her clothes.

Chapter Thirteen

Thursday–To the Bank They Go

Nora had reservations about leaving her grandchildren alone with two of the thugs, but she had no choice. She prayed these hoodlums wouldn't hurt the kids in her absence. She briefly hugged them both before going upstairs to change into her suit. They both gave her a forlorn smile as she walked away.

"Can I take a quick shower before I get dressed?" she asked Nails.

"Make it quick. And don't try any tricks."

She got her clothes from the closet and fresh undies from the dresser. While alone in the bathroom, she was so tempted to get the gun out of the panty liner box, but she didn't know how to get it out of the bathroom without Nails noticing it. Damn! She should've brought in a purse. She could've slipped it inside. There went a perfect opportunity.

Quickly showering, brushing her teeth, using the john, she dressed in her mauve suit with a white blouse, put on a bit of makeup—especially concealer on her injured eye, and combed her hair. When she came out of the bathroom, Nails was sitting on the bed, watching the bathroom door. She turned to look at him as she walked toward the closet. "I'm going to get my shoes and purse from the closet." She opened the closet door and found matching shoes and a purse she hadn't given to Primo. Turning around, she asked Nails, "Are you going with me to the bank? If so, why don't you pick out some clothes to wear from the other closet?"

"I'll do that after you come out of your closet. I need to make sure you don't take anything out of there that you shouldn't."

"Okay. Suit yourself. You know, everything was cleared out of it already when Primo shadowed me."

He just stared at her.

She set her handbag on the bed while she dropped the shoes on the floor. As she sat down to put on the shoes, Nails came over and checked the inside of the purse. A wave of relief enveloped her, knowing she hadn't taken the purse into the bathroom with her and put the gun into it. Now she was sure he would've examined it when she exited the bathroom.

After putting on her shoes, she waited on the bed while Nails found a pair of khaki pants and a blue polo shirt to wear. He gathered the clothes, and they went downstairs. At the bottom of the stairs, she stood in front of the hall closet. "I need to get my wallet from my purse that's in here."

Nails pushed her aside, looked in the closet, and came out with her everyday purse that she kept on the closet floor when she was home. He opened it up and looked inside for anything he didn't want her to remove. Seeing no type of weapon, he handed the purse to her. She removed her wallet, her keys, and a small packet of tissues and slipped them into the other purse, then tossed the everyday one back onto the closet floor.

Nails ordered, "Go back in the livin' room and wait for me to change my clothes."

He watched as she walked into the living room and sat on the couch.

"Well, look at Miss Rich Bitch. Ain't she somethin'?" She knew Primo was only saying this to taunt her. She didn't respond to his snide remark.

She had to gather up the identification documents needed for the bank. "Primo, I need to get all the paperwork to take with me. I know you don't trust me to accomplish it on my own. Do you want to follow me to be sure I don't grab a weapon somewhere?"

He gave her an evil stare again but got out of the chair. She grabbed the bank statements from off the table and went in search of her ID documents.

She thought she might need proof of her residence. No water bills existed since their property had its own well and septic system. An electric bill should suffice. It was in both Dave and her names. Those bills were kept in one of the office filing cabinets. She entered the office and approached that cabinet, momentarily glancing at the exposed safe on the wall and regretting not being able to access the money and jewels inside. Maybe it was for the best. All their stocks and bonds were in the safe. Who knew what Primo would want her to do with them?

She took out the most recent electric bill from its file. Just to be sure, she also removed a copy of the paid statement of their county taxes. This too had both their names as the owners of the property.

Next, she went to the supply cabinet and retrieved a manila pocket folder to hold all the documents she had collected. Approaching the desk and taking a sheet of paper from the note pad and a pen from the top of the desk, she wrote the amount she planned to withdraw from the bank, $350,000, and put it in the folder.

Primo followed her out of the office, staggering slightly in his drunkenness. She sat on one of the side chairs, opened her purse, and took out her wallet, making sure she had her driver license and her bank card. She had other forms of identification in the wallet in case the bank requested more evidence of her identity.

While examining the contents of her wallet, she remembered the few hundred dollars in cash in the money section. Removing the cash, she addressed Primo, "I forgot I had this money. Do you want it or can I use it to buy the groceries today?"

"How much you got there?"

"About two-hundred-fifty and some change."

"Well, since I'm gonna be a rich man soon, you can use that to buy some food for me and my boys." He nodded his head and peered toward Tonto. "I'm such a kind dude, ain't I, Tonto?"

"Yes, you are, Primo. You sure are a nice guy." Tonto said it as if he really meant it, which from his point of view, he probably did.

Nails came out of the bathroom as Nora was replacing her wallet into the purse. She was surprised how a change of clothes actually made him look less like a villain than the dark, dismal black apparel he had been wearing. The outfit fit him fairly well. Maybe the pants were a little long. Dave was very tall. Nora commented, "You clean up pretty good, Nails."

Primo interrupted. "Quit the chatter and get the hell out of here. Get that money business rolling, then get some decent food in this joint. No tricks, old woman. You know what will happen if you try anything."

She walked toward the door to the garage with Nails right behind her. "I know, supreme master, I know."

He yelled back at her as Nails closed the door, "Bitch!"

In the garage, she pressed the fob to unlock the doors of her minivan. Opening the driver door, she slid in behind the steering wheel. As she was fastening her seatbelt, Nails got in the passenger seat. He sat there for a few seconds, then said, "What are you waitin' for, bitch? Let's go."

"Not until you put on your seatbelt. You should know I don't want to be stopped by the police for any reason."

He grumbled something she couldn't hear, but he did fasten the belt.

She turned on the car, pressed the garage door opener, and coasted out when the door was completely open. As she exited, she glimpsed at the huge black van parked on the other side of the double drive. She felt a tinge of regret. It was undoubtedly packed full with her belongings. But they were just things. At that moment, she was concerned more about the two young lives in her house than anything in that van.

At the end of her long driveway, she pulled the minivan onto Smith Garner Road, drove the speed limit to West Middletown Road, and turned left on North Twelfth Street. No conversation between her and Nails took place during the entire trip into Sebring. When she reached the bank, she drove her vehicle around to the back of the building and parked against the blank wall. They got out of the minivan and walked to the entrance.

To her surprise, Nails opened the door for her. She

gave him a stunned look and a smile. He merely shook his head.

Inside, the bank was fairly busy. All five tellers were helping customers. Nora got in the line to await her turn. Nails stood stiffly beside her with his hands clasped behind his back. She assumed his weapon was in his pocket in case he needed it. She hoped to hell it wasn't visible to anyone in the bank.

When her turn in line came, she and Nails advanced to a teller to her right, a middle-aged woman dressed in a floral blouse, her strawberry blonde hair closely cropped. "Good morning. How can I help you?"

Nora stood in front of the Plexiglas window opening while Nails rested his forearm on the side counter. Clearing her throat, she responded, "Good morning. I'd like to withdraw a large sum of money from my savings account. I was told I have to fill out some type of form. I think I have all my needed identification documents."

"How much do you want to withdraw, ma'am?"

Nora didn't want to say the amount out loud, fearing someone nearby might hear her. She and her grandkids were in enough trouble already with the three gunmen now in her life. She didn't need some other deadbeat targeting her. She removed the small note from the folder with the amount of $350,000 written on it and handed it to the teller.

The woman appeared startled when she read the note. "Oh, uh, okay. Uh, what is your name?"

Nora handed her the copy of the savings account statement, figuring the teller could see her name, the account number, and also the balance in the account.

The teller examined the statement, and this time

she was able to keep her expression neutral. She looked up at Nora after her brief inspection. "Please have a seat in the waiting area. I'll get a bank representative to assist you with this transaction."

About a half-dozen upholstered, muted blue patterned chairs and a few small, wood tables rested on a patterned blue area rug to the right of the teller section. Nails and Nora sat on two adjacent seats. Four glassed-in offices were across from them on the other side of the lobby. Nora noticed a man in the end office pick up his phone. He glanced out into the lobby area. Their eyes casually met when he looked her way. He hung up the phone, got out from behind his desk, tucked his shirt firmly into his trousers, and calmly walked out of his office toward them. "Mrs. Mitchell?" He held out his hand. "I'm Clyde Rutherford, the branch manager. Please come into my office so I can assist you."

She shook his hand in acknowledgement, and she and Nails followed him to his office.

Mr. Rutherford was a fairly young man, perhaps in his early forties. He wore no jacket, but his beige shirt was crisp and tailored complemented by a brown and tan paisley tie. When Nails and Nora entered his office, they sat on the two chairs in front of his desk. Nora made her introductions. "Mr. Rutherford, I'm Nora Mitchell, and this is my nephew, Bobby Mitchell. I'd like to withdraw a substantial amount of money from my savings account." At least she didn't choke when she introduced Nails.

Rutherford leaned back in his chair. "Mrs. Mitchell, are you aware there is a protocol for withdrawing large sums of money?"

"Oh, yes sir, I am. I called earlier this morning to find out what I needed and how to proceed. I have with me my identification to verify who I am." She removed all the documents from the folder and handed them to Rutherford.

He took them from her and looked over each one, including the savings account statement. It took him a few minutes to compare all the documents with each other. When he was done, he returned the papers to her. "I assume you also have personal ID with you, Mrs. Mitchell?"

"Yes, I do." She reached in her purse, retrieved her wallet, removing her driver license and bank card and handing them to him.

He also looked over these ID cards scrupulously before returning them to her. "It appears all the paperwork is in order. You will now need to fill out and sign our Cash Withdrawal Letter of Indemnification." He reached into one of the drawers of his desk and removed a single sheet document and handed it to her. "If you will take a few minutes to fill out this form, we'll start the procedure for you to get your money. You may be aware that we do not keep enough cash on hand to dispense that amount to you today."

"Yes, I am. However, I hope you can hasten the process as much as possible. My need is time sensitive. I'm buying a vacation home in Costa Rica, which requires me to pay in cash. The house is perfect for my needs, but there are other prospective buyers—some Costa Rican citizens, some foreigners like me. I'm afraid if I don't act quickly, one of these potential buyers will obtain their funds before I do."

Rutherford came forward in his chair, set his

elbows on the desk, and clasped his hands together. "I understand the urgency of the matter for you, but how much time this will take is beyond my control. I'll submit your request immediately after you complete the form, but I can't guarantee the speediness of the transaction. It will take up to four to seven business days to complete it."

She leaned back in her chair and released a disappointed, deep sigh. Even though she expected it, his statement was still very frustrating. It was Thursday. This could mean she and the kids could be stuck in the house being terrorized by Primo and his cronies for a week or even more. They couldn't survive that amount of time. Tempers had flared just in the few hours they'd held them captive. How could they go on for days? They couldn't. Plain and simple. They couldn't do it.

But she had to pretend in front of Rutherford and especially in front of Nails that she was okay with everything and that she had no vital concerns about the time delay. Who cared what Rutherford believed? Although, if he had any hint that she was lying about why she needed the money, his opinion would be a big concern. As for Nails, she was already fretting over how he was handling all this. He would relay his views on the situation to Primo, and Primo, being the hothead that he was, would not be at all obliging. What was she to do? The only thing she could do at that point was to agree with Rutherford's time prediction, fill out the damn indemnification form, and go back home to await Primo's wrath and whatever consequences were in store for them. And desperately come up with a new plan.

She made one final attempt. "Are you sure there's no way I can get it any sooner?"

Rutherford offered her a look of sympathy. "I'm sorry, Mrs. Mitchell, but $350,000 is a rather large sum of money, and it takes time and protocol to accumulate and go through all the bank's channels."

She gave up. "Then I guess I have no choice." She stood up to leave his office. "You'll notify me as soon as the money is available?"

Rutherford also arose from his chair. "Of course. Just fill out the cash withdrawal letter and return it to any of the tellers. I'll see that we get started on this immediately."

She took the form from him and thanked him for his time. She and Nails went back to the lobby, where she filled it out at one of the lobby kiosks. The letter itself was basically just to protect the bank from any liability with the release of that much cash. She returned the form to the same teller with whom she had spoken earlier, asking if she'd give it to Rutherford immediately. Then she and Nails left the bank and walked back to her car at the rear of the building.

In the car, they did not communicate with one another for several minutes. Nails hadn't said much in the bank either. What could he say? He wasn't happy with what he witnessed. Hell, he was looking forward to getting the money and taking off to some paradise island as soon as possible. Maybe even Costa Rica. In all honesty, he was probably as disappointed as she was. But to hell with him. And to the other two tyrants too. She had to come up with another plan. But what??

"That sucks!" Nora suddenly heard Nails say.

"Yes, it does," she agreed. However, she had to act as if this obstacle with the bank was only a minor hiccup. "But that's okay. We can do this."

144

Nails didn't respond immediately. He stared ahead at the road. When he spoke in a deadpan manner, his voice was saturated with frustration and resignation. "Lady, are you dreamin'? This ain't gonna happen."

Chapter Fourteen

Thursday Afternoon

Nails and Nora spoke no more while she drove to the grocery store. They were both extremely discouraged. He wasn't so naive to think that wild scheme of hers would work. Hopeful? Yes. Already envisioning a sandy beach with a cool, alcoholic drink in his hand? Yes. And knowing there was no way on God's green earth Primo would sit still for a week without something tragic happening? Definitely, yes.

At the grocery store, Nails closely followed Nora while she loaded the cart with whatever she thought they'd need for a week's worth of food to provide for seven people, even though she knew in her heart she was only fooling herself. They were never going to use it all. She was merely postponing the inevitable, hoping she could come up with some other plan to get them to safety and end this horrific ordeal.

When she completed her grocery task, the two of them loaded the bags in the back of the minivan and silently got back in their seats for the trip to the house. She was surprised when Nails started to speak. "Look, lady, I'm sorry about all this shit. When me and the boys started out to target you, I didn't expect it would wind up like it did. It was supposed to be just a simple robbery. First, we didn't count on the kids being there.

We figured you'd be alone; we'd take what we could find and be on our way without much hassle from you. We had on our masks; you had no idea who we were; we'd get away scot free."

She couldn't help herself. She began to cry softly but kept her eyes fixated on the road. "Why did you target me? What did you expect?" Her thoughts briefly went back to when the black vehicle had harassed her on her trip back from Zep's Pizza. "Were you guys in that van that tried to kill me?"

He didn't answer right away, but then he acknowledged, "Yeah, that was us."

"Why? What were you trying to accomplish?"

Again, he was silent. At first, she thought he wasn't planning on responding with anything else. But then he shocked her. "Primo wanted to scare you. He figured we'd force you off the road."

"What good would that do him? All I had in my car was pizza and a few dollars in my wallet."

More silence. She waited.

"He figured you'd be scared and do whatever he asked. Then we'd take control of you and your car. You'd take us to your house. We'd rob the place and be on our way. We wouldn't need Deet's help then."

She was dumbfounded. So their crime spree did start the night before. It was merely postponed a day.

She barely heard his next remarks. "Guess he was wrong. You gave us the slip."

Briefly turning her head toward him, she scowled. "You guys were trying to kill me. How would that have helped you?" She shook her head in disgust.

As she thought about what he'd said regarding her being alone, she wondered about another point. "If you

147

thought I was alone, what the hell did Deet tell you guys? He knew the kids were with me."

Silence for a while.

"Yeah, well, we didn't know they were there when we followed your car. It wasn't until later that night after you ditched us. We were at Tonto's crib with Deet, smokin' weed and drinkin' beer. That girlie texted Deet and told him she was stayin' at your place for a couple a weeks, and maybe one day he could come out with their other friends and spend the day. So when Primo found out those kids were there, he decided to go through with the robbery anyhow, but using Deet this time. He was really psyched about doin' this job."

They were both quiet again until she reiterated her prior question. "So why me?"

"Well, uh, the other day, Deet was talkin' to Tonto, and he told him about this friend of his who had a rich grandma. Guess he told Tonto your old man died and you were all alone out in the middle of nowhere. When Tonto told Primo, we started watchin' your house. Primo figured you'd be an easy mark, you being old and all."

Still looking at the road, she chuckled ironically and sarcastically replied, "Yeah, you left evidence of that back in the woods."

He made no comment.

"What about my doggie door? Was that part of your plan?"

He wavered. "Yeah."

"What happened?"

"Primo thought since Deet was a small kid, he could fit through it and open the door for us. That didn't work either."

"I guess not! He ruined my doggie door."

"Then Primo came up with Deet comin' to the front door. We figured since you knew him you'd let him in. And Primo thought an old lady and two kids wouldn't be a match for three guys like us with guns."

She was angry, but she was at least satisfied that Nails gave her some explanation for this crime spree. Apparently, these sons of bitches did these things on a regular basis. While he was revealing things, she tried to keep him talking. "Do you guys have real jobs? Or do you make your living stealing from other people?"

"Yeah, we work."

"What kind of work do you do?"

"Tonto and Primo are janitors at the hospital. I work for the city collecting trash."

"So you get a paycheck and work hard for your money. Then why do you find it necessary to take things that don't belong to you? Don't you think those people worked hard for their money too?"

That was the wrong thing to say. Someday she'd learn to keep her cynical comments to herself. He was angry. "Just drive, bitch!"

Their conversation ended. Nora had gotten some answers, but as she drove, she kept wondering why Nails would reveal these things to her. Had he and Primo already discussed her fate when this was over? And the kids? The thought was daunting. It would mean whatever she did, whatever the kids did, really didn't matter. Those men couldn't let them go no matter what. She came to the conclusion that inevitably Primo planned to kill the three of them.

At her property, she drove the minivan into the garage, and Tonto came out to help with the groceries.

They carried the food into the house. Under Tonto's watchful eye, she put everything away before going into the living room to explain to Primo what had transpired at the bank. It was obvious that Nails had already done that duty for her. Primo did not look happy. He was sitting on the couch, all stretched out. In his hand was a half-full glass of Jim Beam. At least that was what it looked like. Possibly it was a root beer or cola. But before she had gone to the store, she didn't have any soft drinks left in the house. Therefore, her first guess had to be the correct one. No way would this man be drinking pop when there was a cabinet full of liquor in Dave's office.

"So, bitch, do I get my money tomorrow?" His words were slurred. Nora wondered how many drinks he had consumed while they were gone.

She looked over at Nails, sitting on one of the side chairs. He immediately turned away from her glance. Yep. He already talked to Primo.

"Obviously, Nails has told you our success story. You know what happened."

"Yeah," he garbled. "I know you think I'm gonna wait a week to get my money." His voice got louder with each word he spoke.

"That's not exactly what the banker said." She tried to explain in more detail. "He said it would take four to seven business days, which means it could be ready by Tuesday. He also said he would stress the urgency of the situation, so there's a possibility we could get it even by Monday. *Maybe*."

Nails didn't add any agreement or disagreement to her explanation.

"Bitch! I ain't gonna be stuck in this hell hole with

150

you idiots over a weekend, not knowin' when I'll get my friggin' money. You think I'm a fool? You got to think of something else, and you'd better do it fast."

She sat on the chair between the kids, feeling defeated. They both gave her concerned looks. She peered down at her lap, closed her eyes, grabbed her head with both hands, and concentrated.

Okay. Primo won't wait until next week for the money. No surprise there. Can't say I blame him. If I were in his shoes, I wouldn't go along with that lame-brain scheme either. Too much could happen. But what else can I do? I can't open that damn safe. Why not? Dave wouldn't have changed the combination without telling me. I know he just wouldn't do that. So what did I do wrong? What if I look at the instructions? They should be in the file cabinet with the purchase receipt. I'm sure we still have it. That'll be the first thing to do. And if I get the safe open and they are satisfied with taking its contents, what then? We've seen their faces; we know their real names. They won't let us go, knowing we can identify them. I could promise I won't give them up to the police, but Primo is too smart to believe that. And the things Nails told me verify they plan to get rid of us. That means if I get the safe open, I have to somehow be prepared to fight them. I've got to get my hands on my gun. And the iron pipe. And the dogs.

She took her hands away from her head and looked at Primo. "Before you tie me up again, can I change my clothes and get something to eat? There wasn't enough of the breakfast this morning for all of us. I bought meat and cheese for sandwiches and some potato salad and fruit. I'll fix them for all of us."

Dismissing her, Primo roared, "Yeah, yeah, bitch. Go change your friggin' clothes." He was deep in thought about the whole situation. "Then get your ass down here and fix us some more food."

She went upstairs with Tonto following her. Good. He'd be a little easier to fool than Nails. She took out a pair of cargo shorts from her bureau. They had several deep pockets on each side in which she could hide things. She selected a T-shirt and socks from other drawers and walked to the closet to get shoes. She wanted it to appear that she had a lot in her arms.

To get to the bathroom where she planned to change clothes, she had to walk by the bed. On her way, she purposely dropped one of her shoes, tossing it slightly under the bed. She reached down to pick it up, also searching for the twelve-inch iron pipe while grabbing for her shoe. Her hand touched the cold metal. She quickly grasped the fallen shoe and the pipe while her back faced Tonto and slipped the pipe under the clothes in her arms. Holding everything tightly to her body, she marched into the bathroom.

As she was closing the door, Tonto yelled, "Hey, lady. You got to leave that door open a little bit so I can hear what you're doin' in there."

"Okay." She left it open about two inches. Quickly changing her clothes, she slipped the pipe under her shirt into the waistband of her shorts on the left side. Then she quietly opened the linen closet, rummaged in the sanitary napkin panty liner box for the revolver. She found it and slipped the gun into the deep pants pocket on her right side, making sure the pocket flap covered it. The shorts had a drawstring as well as an elastic waistband. She tightened the drawstring so the pants would stay around her waist more securely. Then she had to get by Tonto without him detecting the extra weight she was carrying.

He noticed nothing unusual as they left the bedroom. The pipe was cutting into her ribs when she walked down the stairs. She had to stand up as straight as possible. Tonto followed right behind her, but he didn't seem to be aware of her strange posture.

When she walked into the living room, Primo was dozing on the couch. The kids were also having a difficult time keeping their eyes open. Nails was alert and watching all of them.

"Primo, I'm going to fix the sandwiches now. Is it okay if Sonya helps me?"

He opened his eyes. "Yeah, yeah. Tonto, cut the brat loose."

Nora waited while Tonto cut the tape from Sonya's hands and feet. Then Sonya and Tonto followed her into the kitchen. When the dogs heard the sounds of people nearby, they started barking, whining, and scratching at the door. Sonya gestured toward the utility room with her right arm. She asked Tonto, "Can I feed them and give them some water? Maybe can I let them outside for a little bit?"

Tonto looked confused. His head turned toward Nora then back to look at Sonya. "Uh, I don't know. Lemme go ax Primo. You guys gotta come with me."

They turned around and walked back to the living room with Tonto and his gun right behind them.

"Hey, Primo, okay if this chick feeds those dogs? Can she let 'em outside?"

Primo jerked upright on the couch, wrinkling his face. "Hell, no, she can't take them outside! Let 'em piss and shit in the room. That'll give you brats somethin' to do when we're outta here."

Sonya conceded, "Can I at least feed them and give them some water?"

"Yeah, yeah. Do it quick. Then get back in that damn kitchen and get my sandwich. I'm hungry."

Back in the kitchen, Nora got out the dog dishes, a can of wet food, and the container of dry food. As she bent down to fill the dishes with the kibble, the pipe stabbed her under the arm. She flinched, but Tonto didn't notice. She was more careful after that when she portioned out the food into the three dishes.

Sonya opened the canned food and divided its contents between the bowls, mixing it together with Gordy getting a smaller amount than the other two dogs. The dogs were normally fed in the utility room, so they expected to eat there. Their water bucket would be filled from the utility sink in the room.

Sonya, Nora, and Tonto entered the utility room. The dogs went wild with barking, howling, and jumping. They were upset and hungry. They leaped on Nora and Sonya and tried to get to the food. Luckily, they ignored Tonto. Sonya gave Cleo and Amos their dishes. After Nora placed Gordy's food near him, she rinsed and filled the almost empty water bucket with fresh, clean water. They were able to sneak back into the kitchen while the dogs were busy chomping their food.

The stench in the room was almost unbearable. It smelled like an overflowing toilet, but there was nothing Nora could do about it. The disgusting odor permeated into the kitchen, which also was beyond her control. She didn't know what Primo would do if it became intolerable to him.

After she left the utility room, she remembered something important. On a low shelf sat a plastic container filled with sports equipment—baseballs, football, baseball mitts, a badminton set, and a few other outdoor activity items. One thing that wasn't in the bin was a baseball bat because it was too big and stood next to the shelving unit. If they were able to make an attempt at an escape, it would be a very handy item to grab.

Planning how they could get out of captivity was still on her mind when she went back into the kitchen. She and Sonya stood at the sink washing their hands. As her granddaughter turned on the faucet, Nora leaned close. "I have an idea. I'll try to tell you about it when we get back in the living room and things quiet down."

Tonto yelled, "Hey, no talking."

Nora finished washing her hands. Sonya nodded her head in approval, and they began the task of making the sandwiches.

Nora took the lunchmeat and cheese from the refrigerator. Sonya got out the bread and started laying slices out on the counter to put on the spreads. Nora turned to her. "Sonya, go see what those men, Deet, and Collin want on their bread—mayo, butter, ketchup, mustard, or whatever."

Sonya left the open loaf of bread on the counter and walked toward the living room. When Tonto chose to follow Sonya, Nora removed the iron pipe from her waist and quickly thrust it into the bottom cupboard where she kept the dog food. If these thugs were going to look for food, they wouldn't choose to scavenge through any of the dog food. She was casually taking the potato salad out of the refrigerator when Sonya and Tonto returned to the kitchen.

"Did you get their orders, hon?" Nora asked Sonya.

"Yeah, I'll take care of it."

After they made the sandwiches, Sonya placed them on paper plates while Nora dished out dollops of the potato salad.

Sonya handed Tonto his plate and grabbed Nails', Deet's, and Primo's. Nora took Collin's, Sonya's, and her own. As they entered the living room, Nails unbound Deet's and Collin's hands so they could eat, and everyone's plates were distributed.

Nails placed his plate on the side table. "We got some more cold beer at the grocery store. I'm gonna get us some."

Primo approved. "Good thinkin'. If we have to put up with all this shit around here, we need some decent brews."

"May I go with him to get us some cans of pop?" Nora asked.

"Yeah, yeah." Primo shooed her away with his left hand while biting into the sandwich in his right hand. His gun lay beside him.

Nails followed Nora into the kitchen, and she waited behind him while he removed the cold beers from the fridge. He moved aside to allow her to take out four cans of pop. Opening his beer, he took a swig and said, "I hope you come up with some other plan soon 'cause Primo's not gonna be patient much longer."

"I know. I know. I do have a couple of ideas, but thanks for the warning." She didn't say anything for a couple of seconds while Nails took another swallow of his beer. "You know, Nails, I don't think you're as bad a guy as you want us all to believe."

Nora was shocked to see the change on Nails' face from a blank look enjoying a swig of beer to a frightening, evil mask. "Lady, don't think you know me. You don't know what I'm capable of. Now get your ass in that living room."

Chapter Fifteen

Late Thursday Afternoon

After lunch and a bathroom break, the captives
were bound back up. Surprise, surprise.

"Okay, bitch. I'm gonna take a little nap on the
couch," Primo declared. "That means you have a couple
of hours to think about a better plan on how you're
gonna get me my money. I'm not satisfied with your
current idea, and I'm losing my patience. If you don't
have one by then"—he stretched his body out on the
couch—"we're gonna cause a lotta pain around here,
starting with that kid." He pointed to Collin as he rested
his head on the soft arm of the couch.

Nora knew she was running out of time. After they
bound her back up, she tried very hard to concentrate
on a new plan. Time passed. Maybe about fifteen or
twenty minutes.

Primo had allowed Deet's hands to remain free,
Deet had quickly removed the tape from his ankles and
trudged over to a corner chair, frowning while gazing
out the front window. Nails and Tonto sat in other
chairs behind the captives. Nora couldn't tell if they
were dozing or if they had their guns targeted at their
backs.

Thankfully, since they were never gagged, Nora
could communicate with the kids in whispers—as long

as they were careful.

Nora first turned to Sonya and leaned as close as she could. "I hid an iron pipe in the cabinet with the dog food. If we can find a way out of this horror, you or Collin grab it. Also, the baseball bat is in the utility room, next to the bin with all the other sports equipment."

"What are you planning to do, Granny?"

"I'm not sure yet, but it's going to be soon. You heard Primo's threat." Nora didn't want to give her granddaughter any hint that she thought they planned to kill them after they got her money.

Nora then leaned toward Collin and told him the same thing she had told Sonya. He looked at her in surprise. "How did you get the pipe?"

"When I changed my clothes, I purposely dropped my shoe near the bed and picked it up at the same time as the shoe. My back was to Tonto, so he didn't see the pipe. Then when I was in the bathroom, I hid it in my waistband. When Sonya and I were fixing lunch, I snuck it in the cupboard with the dog food."

Collin nodded his head. "Smart move, Granny."

Now that the kids knew about the potential weapons, Nora concentrated on a plan of escape. All kinds of scenarios went through her head. None of them seemed to be possible. Sure, she had the loaded gun in her pocket, but it was useless to her as long as she was confined to the chair. Plus, each of these brutes also had a gun.

It had been quite some time since she had done any target practice. Would she still be able to handle the gun? She was positive she'd have the courage to shoot it. No doubt in her mind, these weasels were going to kill her and her grandchildren. She realized, above all, her being able to shoot the gun would be a moot point if she couldn't get her hands and legs free. The only times they were not bound to the chairs were when they were ordered to raid her house for their contraband, fixing food for the beasts to eat, or being allowed to go to the bathroom. In each case, one of those men constantly followed them. Well, maybe not in the bathroom. But could she come out of the bathroom fast enough to get the draw on whoever had the gun on her? Of this she was very doubtful.

She closed her eyes and took deep breaths. She had to come up with something. But what? As her mind tossed ideas in her head, for some reason, she began to picture the safe in Dave's office. She thought about how she tried to open it: Turn the dial left past fifty four times—*wait a minute*.

She suddenly realized Dave never changed the combination at all. She was so nervous both times she tried to open the safe that she completely messed up how to move the dial. She closed her eyes and visualized the instructions in the booklet they kept with the paperwork on the purchase of the safe. "Turn the dial counter-clockwise *four times*. Stop on your first number."

That's where she'd made her big mistake. She was supposed to *stop* on fifty on that fourth time, not pass it up. Lordy! How could she have been so stupid? Now *she* should be called Dumbass instead of Tonto. And all this time stressing out and creating havoc because of her stupidity. She would look at the instruction booklet to verify it, but she was positive that was what she had done wrong. Bearing that in mind, she had also turned to the other numbers in the combination too many times. What a fool!

Okay. At least she could fix that part of their dilemma. They no longer had to worry about the bank getting the money in time. Hopefully, if Primo got his hands on what was in the safe, he'd be content. She wasn't sure how much cash was in there, maybe fifty or seventy thousand or so, but her jewelry alone was at least worth fifty thousand or more.

Dave's knife collection was probably worth another fifty grand. And the stock and bond certificates? Dave talked about having the brokerage firm hold them, but he never proceeded with that idea. How could he have guessed something like this would ever happen? Surely, if they were stolen, Nora could contact the broker so they somehow would stop the thieves from cashing them in. She needed that chance to find out.

Thus, she determined that opening the safe meant a big part of their dilemma would be solved. But what good would that do? As soon as it was open and those demons collected its contents, Nora, Sonya, and Collin would be killed.

Her mind was blank while she stared at Primo's snoring in rhythm with saliva drooling onto her couch. If it weren't for this man, they'd probably be in the pool at that very moment thinking about what to have for dinner. Or she might have been on the porch watching the kids play in the water while she thought about what she would do for the rest of her life. Or perhaps they'd be hiking in the woods, admiring the wildflowers, maybe picking a bouquet for the dinner table. But as she stared at that despicable man, she dwelled on the fact that he took those things away from them.

That man also deprived her of her time to grieve properly. She shouldn't be thinking about how to save her own life and that of her grandchildren. She should have this time to remember Dave—the times they shared, the life they'd made for each other and their children. Instead, there she was—bound up in her own living room with her own duct tape, trying to figure out how she could keep her and the kids from dying within the next few hours.

Suddenly, her cellphone rang from inside her shorts' pocket. The kids looked at her. Tonto and Nails swiftly arose from their chairs and came around toward her. Nails demanded, "Tonto, hurry. Cut her hands loose."

Tonto grabbed the knife from the table and cut the duct tape, also nicking Nora's wrist in the process. She had no time to worry about that minor injury. She reached in the pocket on her right side and pulled out her phone. In a voice as calm as she could make it, she answered, "Hello, Amy. Are you already finished with work for the day?"

"Oh, no. I was just checking in to see how things are going and to check with the kids to see what they wanted me to get at the store. What have you all been up to?"

Nora needed to quell her trembling voice. Primo was now awake and staring daggers at her. "Oh, we spent most of the day in the pool. Actually, they're still out there."

"That's a shame. I wanted to talk to them."

"I'll tell them to call you back when they come inside. By the way, we went to the grocery store this morning. The kids wanted to pick out their own things. So you won't have to stop for us tomorrow." So many lies she had to tell.

"You already went to the store? Mom, are you sure you were up to that?"

"It's fine, dear. It gave me something to do. And they had a good time helping me."

"Well, okay then. I guess tomorrow night I'll just stop to get us carryout for dinner on my way to your place."

Considering all the turmoil, Nora completely forgot about Amy's plan to come out after work on Friday. She had to think of something fast. "Oh, uh, dear, I guess I forgot to tell you. Brian called last night. He invited us over to his place. We're going to the beach and the amusement park. He thought the kids would enjoy it. Marcus will be home for the weekend too, so Sonya and Collin can spend some time with their cousin. They don't get that opportunity too often anymore."

As expected, Amy sounded stunned at Nora's decision. *"What? You're driving up to Brian's place? I thought you didn't want to go there."*

"I changed my mind. We'll just stay the weekend. I should've told you last night, but I forgot."

"I don't know what to say to this change. I'm just so…so surprised."

Nora had to think fast. She needed to give Amy some kind of hint that everything was not what it seemed. Something to convince her to get them help. "You know when I talked to Brian after Dad's funeral, I told him I'd be out as soon as possible. And Lisa said she couldn't wait for my visit." Big lie!

"Mom! What are you talking about? That's not how it went down at all."

"Yes, dear. I knew you'd think it was a good idea. Talk to you later. Love you."

Primo motioned her to finish the conversation. She abruptly hung up the phone. Before putting it in her pocket, she noticed that the battery was very low. Nothing she could do about it. She moved her hands behind the chair to be re-bound, hoping that Amy realized that something was terribly wrong.

"Good job, old woman." Primo's grin was more of a smirk when he lay back down on the couch.

After a few minutes, things settled down again. Nora waited until she heard Primo snoring, knowing then he was back asleep. She also heard muffled sleep sounds coming from behind her. She tried to turn her head to check on the other captors. She was able to see Deet near the picture window. He had his head resting against the back of the chair with his eyes closed and his mouth wide open. He was asleep. She turned her head to the other side and looked behind her. Tonto was on that side, but she couldn't see his face. Nails must've been directly in back of her. She saw no part of him. She first signaled to Sonya on her right, whispering, "Can you see if either Tonto or Nails is asleep?"

Sonya stretched to look behind her. "I can't see Tonto. Nails seems to be dozing. His gun is on his lap with his hand holding it loosely."

Nora nodded her head and turned to Collin. "Can you see Tonto? Is he asleep? Can you see his gun?"

Collin looked to his right, stretching to focus on Tonto. "His chin is on his chest. His gun is in his hand, but it's dangling from his fingers. I think he's asleep."

"Good," Nora mumbled. "We can make some plans."

Both Collin and Sonya came alert and leaned close to Nora. "Okay, here's what I want you two to do. I'm not sure which of you is the strongest. Collin, you're a boy, and usually boys are stronger than girls, and you're tall for your age. But, Sonya, you're older and for your size you're pretty tough, too. The duct tape on your wrists and ankles will stretch. I'm sure if we had enough time, we could wiggle out of the ones binding our hands. But once I get started on my plan, I don't know how much time we'll have. So, if possible, here's what I want you to do."

Nora took a deep breath. "When I was trying to open our safe, I made a huge miscalculation. I was so nervous I wasn't thinking straight. While sitting here, I realized my mistake. I was turning the dial all wrong. I'm going to verify this with the instruction manual, but I'm pretty sure I'm right. What I'm going to do when Primo wakes up is to admit this to him and ask him if I can try once again to open the safe. He doesn't want to wait around for days for the money in my bank account, so I'm hoping he'll be content with what is in the safe. I don't know if he'll go for it. Cross your fingers that he will. If he agrees, he'll get one of the thugs to cut the tape off my hands and feet, and we'll go into Grandpa's office so I can try again on the safe."

She paused and took another breath. "Your job while I'm in that office—I'll try to go as slow as possible—is to work your hands loose from the tape. Maybe while I'm gone, one of you can say you have to go to the bathroom. One of those jerks will have to free your hands and feet. When you come back from the

165

bathroom, instead of just putting your arms around the chair and crossing your wrists like I've been doing each time, put your hands behind your back but place your wrists *parallel* to one another." Sonya and Collin both nodded their heads. "After they are taped, this will create more space to move your wrists and hands. Then concentrate on breaking them loose by twisting, turning, separating, however possible."

They both nodded their heads again to show they understood.

"There is that possibility they'll refuse to allow either one of you to go to the bathroom. That's why I think both of you should immediately try to loosen the tape on your hands and your feet. The sides and legs of these chairs have a ridge going down them. Use that ridge to your advantage. While they're asleep is the perfect time to do this. It's best if I don't attempt to get loose since I'm hoping to be unbound by one of them so I can open the safe."

She looked from one to the other. "Any questions so far?"

Collin asked, "What if we can get them loose, but you didn't get the safe open yet?"

"Then just hold your wrists together as if they were still bound. Same thing with your feet. It's doubtful they'll be looking carefully at your hands and feet. They'll be too anxious to find out what is in my safe."

"Okay, that's what I'll do." he replied.

Sonya tilted her head, twisting her mouth to one side. "So we get loose, what then?"

Her grandmother knew she'd have to get to the scary, unpredictable part. She took an even bigger breath than before and glanced down at her pocket. "I have a gun in my pocket."

Both kids' mouths flew open and their eyes bulged out like bubble gum. Sonya had a hard time controlling her voice. "How did you get *that,* Granny?"

"I'll explain once we're out of this predicament, but I wanted to tell you what I plan to do with it." Again, she glanced at both of them. "When I get the safe unlocked, I'm sure Primo will not let me open its door. He's going to want to make sure there's no gun inside the safe. Plus, he'll be so anxious to get his hands on the money and jewels in there that I think he'll shove me out of the way, which is what I want him to do. My revolver is fully loaded. Your grandfather and I practiced shooting it, so I'm prepared. I'm going to take it out of my pocket as soon as Primo puts his face into the safe."

Collin interrupted, "Don't you think he's going to have his gun too?"

"Oh, I'm sure he will, but he won't be expecting *me* to have one. I'm planning on catching him off guard."

Sonya's eyes were still wide open, the bluish irises glistening. "Are you gonna shoot him?"

Nora wasn't sure what she'd do. She just knew she'd do whatever she had to in order to get away from these men. "I don't know, Sonya. I guess it depends on what Primo does."

The three of them were quiet. Nora let the kids think awhile to give what she had said a chance to sink into their brains. But she had more to tell them. "I'm not going to know if you two will be able to break free. I'm counting on it, but if you can't, I still have the gun. As for what you should do, I told you where I hid the iron pipe and where the baseball bat is located. These are great defense weapons. As are the dogs. So your job is to try to get your hands on the weapons and release the dogs. If I don't shoot Primo, I'll at least shoot the gun. That will cause Nails and Tonto to jump to attention. I don't know what they'll do. Run to the office to see about the shot? Come over to you two with their guns at your back? I don't know. This is not a foolproof plan. The three of us have to improvise and adapt to whatever happens around us. So I can't give you any definitive idea on what to do. But if you get loose and if you can get the weapons, run like hell into the woods. Run as far as you can. Probably the best thing would be to run to a neighbor's house. You guys know the woods better than these creeps do, so you have an advantage." She looked at Sonya. "What do you think about Deet? He's an unknown variable. You know him better than I do. Will he help these guys out, with Tonto being his uncle and all? Or will he be a renegade and join forces with us?"

Sonya shook her head. "I honestly don't know, Granny. I never expected him to be a part of this in the first place. I thought he was my friend. The four of us, Kyle, Jenna, Deet, and me, I thought he was one of my *best* friends. So I don't understand why he'd ever do a thing like this."

Disappointed, Nora sighed, "I guess we'll just have to take our chances and keep our eyes on him. At least he isn't holding a gun."

The three leaned back on their chairs, letting all Nora had said sink in. After a few minutes, Collin leaned toward her. "Granny, I think I got a better idea if we get away from these guys."

She knew her plan was far from perfect. Both Collin and Sonya were intelligent kids. What Collin had to say was worth hearing. Sonya also leaned closer.

"What if instead of running into the woods," he asked, "we get to the Jon boat and row out to the middle of Lake Tenawa? That's the only boat around, so they'd have to swim to reach us."

Sonya added, "I know Deet isn't a very good swimmer."

It was a sound idea. The Jon boat was aluminum at fourteen feet long with oars attached to oar locks. Dave and Nora never wanted to get a motor for it. They used it purely for leisure boating, fishing, and exercise, not for speed. It was large enough to fit all of them.

As Nora was thinking, Collin continued. "The dogs will fit in the Jon boat, too. Except Amos might want to swim for a while. He loves the water."

She was beginning to think his plan was better than her own, but she had one concern. "Collin, I think this is a great idea, but one thing I would change. We don't stop in the middle of the lake. I'm not sure the range of their weapons. We should row to the other side. A few houses are over there where we can try to get help."

Sonya had a concern. "Will we be able to get the boat in the water fast enough and row fast enough to get away from their bullets?"

Collin volunteered, "Yeah, with the three of us pushing the boat we can get it into the water really quick. Uh, what about them shooting at us, Granny?"

Nora straightened in her seat. "You two are good swimmers. If they start shooting and the bullets are getting too close, dive underwater. I'll do the same. We'll leave Gordy in the boat. He's small enough that they won't be able to see him. Besides, I don't think they'll try shooting the dogs. They can't identify them or tell the police what happened here."

Sonya came up with another idea. "Once they wake up, why don't you offer to fix them some food? Collin and I will say we aren't hungry. That way we can spend more time wiggling out of the tape."

"Yeah," agreed Collin. "Maybe it'll be darker then, and they'll have a harder time shooting at us."

"Good idea," Nora agreed.

"So that's our plan then?" asked Sonya.

Under the circumstances, Nora believed their plan *could* work. What did they have to lose? They were going to be killed anyhow. They may as well go down fighting. "Yes. That's our plan."

The three of them nodded their heads. There was one issue to consider. Since they were not going to eat, they wouldn't have the duct tape removed from their wrists. As a result, they wouldn't get the chance to hold their wrists parallel for the re-taping. It would be harder for them to break free.

Nora turned to them one more time. "Okay. We'll go with that plan, but you'd better get started loosening that duct tape right now."

Chapter Sixteen

Thursday Evening

Nora wasn't sure what time it was when their wretched hostage takers began to stir from their naps. It was still light outside, but the sun was going down. She had dozed a little in the chair and hoped the kids had a chance to do so also. They had worked diligently to loosen the duct tape binding their hands and feet. They had a long night ahead of them. At least she hoped they'd still be alive to participate in that long night.

Primo was the first of the rogues to awaken. Being that Nora couldn't see Nails and Tonto behind her, from the tone of Primo's voice, those guys were still napping. He bellowed, "Rise and shine, my pretty ones. We have work to do."

The captives heard stirring behind them. Deet sat up straight in his chair, stretching and yawning. Collin and Sonya were alert.

Primo stared at Nora. "Old hag, have you spent my nap time thinking about how to get me my money?" He had that ugly leer on his face. No matter what, this man could never be considered handsome. His features weren't that bad, but that evil, menacing look never left any of his expressions.

"Yes, I have." She wanted more time. It wasn't dark enough outside to aid them in their planned escape. "I was thinking you might want something to eat before I tell you. It's been a long time since lunchtime. I could broil some hamburgers."

Primo looked at his guys. "You men hungry? Want somethin' to eat before we leave this crib?"

Tonto asserted, "Yeah, man. I could go for a coupla burgers with lotsa fixin's."

"Sounds good to me too," added Nails.

Deet said nothing. Perhaps he was afraid to remind Primo he even existed.

Primo got off the couch, extending his big, muscular arms and grabbing his pistol off the cushion. "Yeah, bitch, fix us some burgers. Then we'll get down to business." He walked around the room, extending his legs and looking like a galloping horse. He tapped his buddy on the back. "Unhinge that bitch, Nails."

Nails cut the duct tape—for the last time, God willing. Nora stood up, moving her body, shrugging her shoulders up and down, attempting to dissipate the stiffness in her old joints and bones. When she felt a little less like a crumpled piece of paper, she took their burger orders. Primo, Nails, and Tonto wanted two each with whatever she had to put on them. Deet wanted one with only ketchup. "How about you, Sonya?"

"I'm not hungry, Granny. I'll pass."

Primo focused on Sonya. "What's the matter, chickie? You don't want to ruin that skinny body you got? You think you won't be sexy no more?"

She softly replied while looking at the floor, "I'm just not hungry. That's all." She didn't want to draw attention to the loosened duct tape around her hands and feet. Hopefully, she had been successful in that endeavor.

"I'm not hungry either, Granny. Don't make any for me," added Collin. "I kinda have a stomachache right now."

Those grandkids of hers could think for themselves.

Primo glared at Collin. "Kid, you'd better eat. Who knows? If that old granny of yours doesn't have a plan to give me my money, this might be your last meal." His venomous smirk encompassed his entire face.

Collin snarled, "I'll take my chances."

"Suit yourself, kid." Primo continued pacing around the room with his gun swinging from his hand.

In the kitchen, Nora prepared the burgers, put them on paper plates, and served those three lowlifes. She didn't put Deet in that category because she wasn't sure where he stood. Perhaps within the next hour his true colors would be revealed. Would he help them out, or would he try to harm them like his uncle and so-called friends?

She didn't fix any sandwich for herself. Her stomach was doing flip-flops with the dread of what was ahead for her. Knowing how *she* felt, maybe Collin's stomach issue was real, not only an excuse to direct attention away from the loosened duct tape binding him.

After she passed out the food, she sat in the chair between Sonya and Collin and waited. No one bound her back up. They were too busy feeding their ugly faces. For an instant, she contemplated taking out her Smith & Wesson revolver and firing at them while they ate. None of them had their guns in their hands.

She looked at Sonya and casually pointed her head to the pocket holding her gun. Her intention was to see if Sonya thought she should use it then and not later. Sonya quickly caught her signal and shook her head, indicating to her grandmother not to withdraw it. Maybe she and Collin hadn't loosened their tape enough yet. Maybe she was just too terrified. Nora didn't know. But she stuck to their original plan and didn't take out the gun. After thinking about it, Nora realized there would be no way she could shoot all three villains before at least two of them could retrieve their own weapons and shoot her, Sonya, and Collin. Very bad idea.

Primo finished his hamburgers. "Okay, bitch, whatchu got for me? It's show time!"

Nora cleared her throat. "Here's the thing. I think I was trying to open that safe the wrong way."

He looked very angry. "What? You were tryin' to pull a fast one on me?"

She quickly blurted, "No! No. I was just so nervous with you breathing down my neck. When I had time to think about it, I realized why I couldn't open it. I have a copy of the instructions for the lock in the file cabinet. I want to look at it to verify the procedure. I'm almost positive I was doing it wrong. But not on purpose!"

"*Almost* positive, huh? That ain't good enough."

"I know it isn't. That's why I want to check the instructions. Then I'll be positive."

He was thinking about what she said. He paced around the room a little. Then he stood tall in front of her. If she wasn't intimidated before, as he stood several feet above her, leering down at her, she surely was then. She clasped her hands together to keep them from shaking. Glancing over at Sonya, she saw her eyes filled with tears. She could almost hear Dave talking to her. *Nora Mitchell, you are strong. You can do this. You are capable of doing whatever you set your mind to. Keep your wits about you. Stay calm and confident. You are smarter than these characters. Get a grip on yourself.*

After the silent pep talk from Dave, she stood up as tall as she could, inches from Primo's imposing body. She brushed against him as she turned toward the hallway. "Let's go to the office. I'll show you, and I'll open that safe."

The eleventh hour had arrived. She looked back at Sonya and Collin and nodded her head. In unison, they returned the nod.

Chapter Seventeen

Thursday Night

When she entered the office, Nora went directly to the file cabinet that held all their warranties and appliance instructions. Primo opened the drawer and checked it for a weapon before he permitted her to look for anything inside.

Dave was very organized with all this paperwork. He was organized about everything. Each appliance or apparatus had its own folder, and they were filed alphabetically according to what type it was, not by its manufacturer. The safe's file was the first one behind the "S" tab. Nora pulled out the entire file and took it over to the desk. Primo followed directly behind her, holding his gun. He didn't jam the gun into her back, but it was close. Too close.

Placing the file on the desk, she leafed through the receipt and the warranty to get to the owner's manual. She turned the booklet to the page dealing with opening the combination lock. And there it was. Line Number One. Directly under the picture of the lock dial: *Starting at zero, turn the dial counter-clockwise—to the left— four times. Stop on your first number.*

She knew it! At least she had something going right for a change. She held the page up to Primo. "See. This is what I was looking for. This was my mistake.

Now I know I can open it. I had the right combination. I was just doing it the wrong way."

He briefly looked at the page but didn't bother to read anything. He gave her a slight nudge with the gun. "Let's go then. Get that friggin' safe wide open and give me my money."

Darkness had encompassed the outside, maybe about nine-thirty. She wasn't sure how big the moon was. All that day the skies had been cloudy, threatening rain. She hoped it had stayed that way through the evening. That would definitely be a plus for what they planned.

She approached the safe. Standing in front of it, she wiped the sweat from her hands on her butt—she didn't want to disturb her revolver in her pocket. Taking a deep breath, she proceeded to enter the combination.

She moved the lock indicator to zero, then slowly twisted the dial to the left three times past zero. On the *fourth* time around, she stopped at her first number, fifty. Next, she turned the dial to the right passing her second number, twenty-four, two times before stopping on it on the *third* time around. Then she turned the dial left again passing her third number, thirty-five, once before stopping on it the *second* time. Next, she twisted the dial slowly to the right again approaching zero, hoping for the long-awaited sound of the lock clicking, signifying the safe was unlocked.

Click!

Nora never saw anyone move as fast as Primo did. He shoved her out of the way, and she staggered against a nearby bookcase, bracing herself. She figured his main concern for pushing her away so quickly was the fear that a gun might've been in the safe, and he didn't

177

want her to grab it. Little did he know, the danger wasn't in the safe, but standing a few feet from him.

As she saw him swing open the safe with his left hand and peer into it, she reached into her pocket, pulled out the revolver, keeping it low against her thigh, and released the safety. She held the gun down to her side until she saw his shoulders bend down and his head look deeply into the safe. His gun, then in his right hand, was switched to his left to free his dominant hand for examining the contents of the safe.

When he focused his eyes back into the safe, Nora raised the Smith & Wesson and pointed it directly at him. To her surprise, she held the gun rather steadily. No nerves; calm as a cucumber.

Primo didn't notice what she was doing because he was so riveted, admiring what was inside the safe. The money was in an unlocked cash box bundled by denominations. He opened the box and looked at its contents. The jewels were in a wooden jewelry box with each item wrapped in satin cloth. The stock certificates were in a large folder. A metal box containing Dave's knife collection took up a big portion of the safe's back compartment.

If he planned to examine any of the contents of these containers or bring any of them out of the safe, he needed to free up both his hands and do something with his gun. *Or* he could appoint Nora to remove the containers and the folder. He didn't know it when he turned toward her, but that wasn't going to happen this time. She was tired of being pushed, shoved, and ordered around. No more physical abuse or name calling would she endure. It was *her* turn to be the number one person in *her* house.

He called out to her while his eyes were still observing what was inside the safe. "Hey, bitch!"

She responded, "Yes, Primo, are you referring to me, Nora Mitchell? What do you want?"

"Get over here and take out my stuff."

In her head, she counted to three and then quietly asserted, "No, Primo."

She saw his body stiffen. Then he slightly closed the safe door to look in her direction. He raised his voice. "What do you mean n—?"

He didn't finish his sentence. Over the safe door, he saw her holding the revolver. Oh, how she delighted seeing the look on his face! Wide eyed; open mouth. What had happened to his proverbial demonic look?

As for Nora? She had a genuine, giant smile that reached from ear to ear.

"Wha...what you got there, old lady?" Deep concern seeped into his voice.

"I think you know what I have here, Mr. Priestley. This is my trusty J Frame Smith & Wesson. It's fully loaded. Care to see what she can do?"

He remembered he had his own gun in his left hand. He swiftly switched it to his right and pointed it at her chest. "Put the gun down, bitch."

"No, I won't do that."

"Put it down, I said."

"And I said, no."

They both stood staring at one another. Nora broke the silence. "If you call for your henchmen, I'll shoot you before they can get in here."

For a few seconds, he continued staring at her, apparently debating whether or not to shoot. But Nora took the guesswork away. Knowing she wasn't the greatest marksperson, she aimed for his right shoulder. Two reasons: That was the hand holding the gun, and the second reason; she didn't plan to kill him. If she aimed for his left shoulder, it was very possible she'd miss and hit his heart. Not her intention.

Nora squeezed the trigger. The bullet pierced his right shoulder.

When she shot him, his face finally lost that menacing look it had possessed since he burst into her house. It wasn't fear she saw, but complete and utter surprise. He didn't think she had the balls to do it. Actually, she wasn't sure herself.

But she did it, and pandemonium broke loose. Within seconds, Nails and Tonto barged into the office, guns in their hands but still at their sides, thinking that Primo had fired at Nora. As far as they knew, she had no weapon.

Primo yelled, "The bitch shot me! Shoot her!" His face was turning pale and blood gushed from the wound, dripping down his chest. His gun dropped to the carpet with a thud, and he dropped to his knee.

Since Primo's gun was not an immediate threat, Nora pointed her revolver at Nails and Tonto, who had started to raise their guns toward her. She shouted the proverbial, "Stop, or I'll shoot." They stopped and looked at her with the same expression as Primo had on his face when she shot him.

"I'm not messing around, guys. I know you both have your guns, but you can see, I already shot Primo. I purposefully didn't shoot to kill him, which I could have done. I don't want to kill you boys either, even though I'm sure you don't feel the same way toward me. But I'm mad as hell. You losers came into my house to steal from me things my husband and I worked hard for over many years. You even planned to kill us. I know that because we learned enough about the three of you to put your asses away for a long time. So I'm asking you nicely to drop your guns to the floor and kick them away, or I might not be so kind as just to shoot you in the shoulder. I may be an old bitch, but I'm now an old bitch with a gun."

Primo stooped over, holding his bloody arm with his left hand. "Shoot her, morons. Shoot her."

Nails and Tonto took too long to decide what do to. Nora shot the revolver. The bullet whizzed between their heads, perhaps a half inch from Tonto's ear. She was actually aiming *above* their heads. But, what the hell! Like she said, she wasn't a very good shot.

Her actions and the sound of that bullet crashing into the door behind Nails and Tonto set them off. After being momentarily startled from the shot at them, Nails and Tonto raised their guns to shoot back. She hadn't recovered enough to aim at them, but she had the presence of mind to duck. The bullets soared above her head into the wall behind her.

Before those two scumbags took a second shot at her or she at them, she heard dogs barking. Since she was so preoccupied, the sound took a while to sink into her brain. When Nails raised his gun hand to shoot his next shot, Sonya burst through the doorway bashing him in the back of the head with the iron pipe. Right behind her, Collin, using the baseball bat, pounded on Tonto. Both men were forced to move forward and hunch down to get away from the blows to their bodies.

Nora didn't wait around. She ran past the men and out the door. "Come on, kids. Let's go!"

After the kids made it through the cracked, office door, Nora slammed it behind them, hoping that might slow their captors down a bit. The three of them ran into the kitchen; Nora quickly unlocked the French door, slammed open the porch door, and they ran as fast as they could to the Jon boat on the shore of Lake Tenawa with the dogs barking and scurrying with them. She took a second to pick up Gordy. He'd never be able to keep up with their pace. Nobody took the time to look back to see where the thugs were. They needed to keep running.

Poor Sonya and Collin. They had been awakened so suddenly on Wednesday night when these intruders invaded their grandmother's house that neither of them had taken the time to put on their slippers or shoes before rushing downstairs. Consequently, they were running in their bare feet.

It took the group a few minutes to reach the Jon boat. Nora tossed Gordy into the boat. Cleo climbed in after him. With the kids on one side and Nora on the other, they pushed the boat into the water. Amos waded into the water to swim next to them.

As they climbed into the boat, someone was running toward them. Sonya yelled, "It's Deet!"

Nora took a second to look up. The cool night was very black by then with dark, low clouds overhead. She couldn't tell if Deet was carrying any weapon, and she only had a second to make a decision. He was a scared kid. He didn't have a gun. Okay. She shouted, "Hurry up, Deet." Within a few seconds, he reached the boat.

"Climb in the boat and grab the other oar," Sonya shouted as she took hold of the first oar. Nora pushed the boat deeper into the water and heaved her body over the edge into the boat. Amos started swimming behind them.

"Keep rowing. Fast as you can," Sonya shouted to Deet. He was having a difficult time getting into the rhythm.

Collin squeezed between Deet and Sonya on the middle seat. He grabbed the oar from Deet. "Here, lemme do it, Deet. I've had more practice." Deet shimmied out of the seat and slithered to the one behind them.

The kids rowed with all their strength. The boat moved swiftly toward the middle of the lake. Nora kept looking back to see if the men were out of the house. It didn't take long. Soon she saw a light dancing toward the edge of the lake. One of the men must've either found a flashlight in the house or in their van. Whatever, they were fast approaching the lake.

"Can you row any faster, kids?" Nora shouted. She knew they were doing the best they could. She was just so concerned those monsters' bullets could reach them.

Sure enough, about ten seconds later, Nora felt and heard the flutter of a passing bullet next to her ear. She yelled, "Everybody duck down as low as you can. They're shooting at us!"

Deet scrunched down on the bottom of the boat, hoarding Gordy under him. Cleo was on all fours. Nora pushed her down also. Then she went behind Sonya and Collin. As they rowed, she stretched her body behind them to attempt to protect them from the whizzing bullets. They were making headway. The bullets kept coming, but soon they heard the plopping sound of the bullets falling into the water behind them. They were finally out of their range.

Nora straightened up, turned around, and looked back at the shoreline. The flashlight was stationery for about another half minute. Then it disappeared. The men had retreated.

"Sonya, Collin, let Deet and me take over the oars. The men have gone back to the house. You guys need a rest. Good job! You got us away from the bullets."

Deet and Nora traded places with Sonya and Collin. It didn't matter then if they weren't in sync with their rowing capabilities. Speed wasn't as imperative once the shooting stopped.

Nora and Deet finally achieved some continuity and made more headway toward the opposite side of the lake. All was quiet except for Sonya and Collin's heavy breathing and the lapping of the water as the oars forced it away from the boat. Without losing rhythm, Nora called back to the kids, "How is Amos doing? Does he need to be pulled into the boat?" She felt the boat's movement as one of the kids looked over the side. They pulled Amos into the boat.

"We got him in," Collin said. "He's worn out."

For a while the boat rocked until the kids got settled again and Amos found a spot to rest. His panting added to the sounds of the heavy breathing and the sloshing of the water as Deet and Nora's rhythm returned. No one felt the need to speak.

Nora wasn't sure how far Lake Tenawa was from the banks of her property to the opposite side. It wasn't a huge lake, like Lake Berlin or Lake Milton, but it wasn't a pond either. It took them totally about a half hour or so to get from one shoreline to the opposite side in the Jon boat. She wasn't too familiar with what occupied the other side. From her property, only a wooded area was visible. A few houses were located on Haskell Road, but she didn't know how far from the lake the road was.

Thus, when they pulled the boat onto that opposite bank, Nora was just as ignorant as everyone else what lay ahead of them. The ground was filled with stones—even some boulders—heavy plant growth, and branches. And Sonya and Collin had no shoes. Nora removed her shoes. "Sonya, take my socks. They'll protect your feet a little bit." She questioned Deet, "Deet, do you have any socks on?"

"Yes ma'am." He immediately removed his shoes and handed his socks to Collin.

After putting on the socks, Sonya gazed around the area. "I can't see anything, Granny."

"I know. I can't either. You guys don't have your phones, right?"

Both of them told her their phones were on their bedside tables, where they left them when this madness began. Deet offered, "I have my phone, Mrs. Mitchell."

"Good, I have mine too, but my battery is very low. I'd like to preserve it as much as possible."

"What are we gonna do now, Granny?" asked Collin.

"Well, the first thing I'm going to do is call your mother. Hopefully, my battery will last. If not, I'll have to use yours, Deet."

Deet nodded his head. "Okay."

She took out her phone, was about to press Amy's number, when she realized she had no service. "Damn!"

"Is your phone dead already?" asked Sonya.

"Not yet, but it seems there's no cell service. Probably with all the trees, the water, and those clouds look awfully dark. I don't know. Guess we'll have to try when we get to a better location. So, Deet, how about turning yours on to give us some light?"

Deet took out his phone and activated the flashlight. The eerie light shimmered on the lake water and their faces, making them look pale and ghost-like.

"Okay. Here's our options. We can go back across the lake. The Pemberton family lives about a mile from our property. My only concern with that is we don't know what those thieves are doing. Are they still at my house? If not, where did they go? Are they searching for us? With Primo being shot, are they headed somewhere to take care of his shoulder? And how seriously did you guys hurt Nails and Tonto? Somebody was able to shoot at us. Perhaps they went to the Pembertons, searching for us."

"Gosh! I hope not," offered Sonya. "I wouldn't wish a visit from those guys on my worst enemy. Maybe we shouldn't go back that way."

Nora agreed. "I think you're right. I don't want to meet up with them just when we thought we escaped. Deet, do you have any idea what they planned to do after they robbed us?"

"I don't know, ma'am. They didn't tell me any of their plans. All they wanted me to do was to get them into your house. That's all I know."

Nora remembered Deet was supposed to tell her why he agreed to help the intruders. She also recalled how nervous he had seemed when Sonya first introduced him on Wednesday. "By the way, Deet. Why did you lead them to my house in the first place? Sonya is your friend. Why would you do something like that to her?"

Sonya voiced her displeasure and impatience with Deet. "Yeah, dude. Why did you do it? If it weren't for you, we wouldn't even be in this situation."

"I'm really sorry. I didn't know what they were gonna do. And they made me do it."

"Aw, come on, Deet! How did they *make* you do it? Did they put a gun to your head like they did us?" Sonya scolded while shaking her head.

"Well, no. They didn't do that. Uh, Primo just caught me smokin' a joint and drinkin' beer. He was gonna tell my dad. My dad woulda killed me 'cause he already caught me twice before. He said if it happened again, I was grounded with no phone for the whole summer. What could I do?"

"So then you thought it was just fine for those guys to barge into my granny's house and steal all her stuff and put their guns to our heads?" hissed Sonya.

This argument had gone far enough. They didn't have time to worry about Deet's prior actions. Nora demanded, "Okay, let's stop arguing. We can figure all this out when we know we're safe." She paused. "Back to the plan: If we don't go toward the Pembertons in the boat, the other option is to go on foot through the woods and see what we find. This is no Alaskan forest, so civilization shouldn't be too far away. It won't take too long before we come to a house or Haskell Road. However, Collin and Sonya, you have no shoes. It's going to be really rough on your feet. What do you think, guys?"

Collin spoke, "I think we should get back into the boat and row toward the Pembertons' property. Take our chances those guys are not there. My feet are already sore from running to the Jon boat. I'm not sure I could make it through these woods."

Nora gazed at all their ghostly faces. "Sonya, Deet, what do you think?"

Sonya agreed, "Yeah, my feet really hurt now too. Plus, who knows what we'd be stepping on. I'm sure there's snakes we wouldn't see until we tramped on one, and then it would be too late. If you say the Pembertons are over a mile from your house, if those dudes are still at your house, they won't see us go to the Pembertons. And if they went to the Pembertons, maybe one of us can sneak around to see if their van is in the driveway before we ask them for help."

"Okay, then. That's how we'll work it. Back in the boat, everybody. Sonya and Collin, you take the first rowing. Deet and I will take over when you get tired."

Nora put Gordy into the boat. Cleo and Amos were exploring the woods. She called out for them, and they came sprinting back. The kids helped them into the boat. Then Sonya and Collin got in and climbed into their position to row.

Nora addressed Deet. "Come on, Deet. Help me push the boat deeper into the water."

The two of them shoved the boat away from the bank. Nora scrambled into the front, and Deet heaved himself into the back seat.

Once Nora settled in her seat, she looked across the lake. "Looks like they turned the backyard lights on. I can't make out anything, just the lights."

Sonya and Collin began to row toward the other shore, angling slightly to the left. They were about a quarter of the way across when it started to rain. The clouds had looked threatening and weighty all day. It was light sprinkles at first, but midway across the lake, the rain got heavier. The boat began taking on water, and everyone got soaked. Looking through the downpour, the lights on Nora's property were blurred and fuzzy. Sonya and Collin picked up their pace, and the boat moved forward more rapidly. The noise from the constant rain hitting the lake water sounded almost like thunder until the real thunder boomed. The sky suddenly lit up with piercing streaks of lightning.

Nora bellowed above the multitude of sounds, "Okay, we have to get off the lake. We're sitting ducks for those lightning strikes."

The dogs started to howl. All three were terrified of thunderstorms. Cleo and Amos would always hide behind the furniture, and Gordy would tremble and nuzzle as close to Nora as he could. "Row toward our woods. We'll go into the girl's fort. It's too dangerous on the water. We need to get off it as soon as we can."

Sonya and Collin rowed faster as the torrential rain and lightning fiercely continued. When they were exhausted, Deet and Nora took over. Deet was catching on to the task, and they got a good rhythm going. They made it to the shore in better time than the original trip.

The boat banked where the woods met the lake, away from the house. Reaching the woods on her property put Nora in familiar territory. She knew the way to the fort, as did the grandkids. It was located about five hundred yards into the woods. The terrain was not as rough as on the other side of the lake. Over the years, they had worn paths throughout their woods. A trail at the lake's edge led right to the forts, the girl's the closest.

Everyone got out of the boat. They pulled it onto the rough shoreline. Amos and Cleo jumped out. Nora grabbed Gordy as she whispered, "We have to be very quiet since we don't know if those men are still in the house or what they might be up to. Sound carries at night, but the rain will help muffle any noise. Try to be as silent as possible, anyhow."

They didn't need Deet's cellphone for its flashlight since the path was clearly marked and the lightning strikes helped brighten the way. They crept as silently as possible toward the fort, sloshing in muddy puddles in the trail. It took them about ten or fifteen minutes to reach the girl's fort. The trees helped shield them from the torrential rain to some degree, but they were still very drenched.

At the fort, Sonya and Collin boosted Amos and Cleo up the ladder. Deet followed them. When Nora carried Gordy halfway up the steps, Collin reached down to grab him.

The rain had really cooled the air and their bodies. Nora motioned to the kids. "A couple of old blankets are packed in that plastic container. Get them out to help keep yourselves warm. Some clean rags are in another container on the shelf. You can dry off with them." Nora took out a couple of raggedy towels and dried the dogs off with them. They settled down on the floor of the fort to catch their breath.

Now that they were temporarily out of danger, Nora needed to call Amy and the police. "Deet, can I use your phone now?" He reached in his pocket and handed it to her. She was able to get a signal.

Nora wasn't sure if Amy would answer her phone. Amy normally didn't respond to numbers with which she wasn't familiar. Nora took the chance she would answer this time. She dialed the number. It rang several times, then went to voicemail.

She left a brief message. "Amy, this is Mom. I'm using Deet's phone. Three thieves attacked us in the house a couple nights ago. We escaped, and we're in the woods in your old fort. Send the police."

She hung up and dialed Amy's number again. It rang several times and went to voicemail again. She didn't leave a message that time. She tried again. Same thing. It rang then went to voicemail. On the fifth try, Amy answered, *"Who the hell is this? Stop bothering me."* The phone was abruptly disconnected.

Nora was frustrated. She took out her own phone. It showed no bars. Sometimes a little juice remains in the battery even when it reads dead. She handed Deet back his phone and tried hers. When Amy's phone rang, she picked it up right away. *"Mom?"*

"Amy call the police. We've—"

The phone suddenly lost power. Amy probably called her back, but there was no way she could check. "Give me your phone again, Deet."

He handed her his phone, and she called 9-1-1. Realizing her foolishness, she reproached herself, "Stupid me, I should've done that in the first place. Sometimes I think I'm losing my mind."

"9-1-1, what is your emergency?"

"This is Nora Mitchell. I live at 12544 Smith Garner Road in Smith Township. Three men with guns invaded my home and kept us captive for two days. They stole my jewels, money, and anything of value."

"Mrs. Mitchell. Where are the gunmen now?"

"I don't know. My grandchildren and I escaped and are hiding in the woods on my property."

"Stay where you are. The police are on their way.

They will identify themselves and come into the woods to get you. Please stay on the line with me until they arrive."

"Okay. We're in a pink and purple fort about two hundred yards from the house."

The 9-1-1 operator sounded confused. "*Uh, Mrs. Mitchell, it seems the police are already at your property.*"

How could that be? Even if Amy got the message from Nora's phone before the battery died, the police wouldn't have a chance to get to the house so quickly. "They're already at my house?"

"*Yes. Apparently, someone called about twenty minutes ago to report a possible problem.*"

"What kind of a problem?"

"*I don't know the answer to that. I do know that they are currently on the premise. Let me get in touch with them to update your location. Stay on the line.*"

Very weird. She waited anxiously for the operator to get back to her.

"What's going on?" asked Sonya.

"I'm not sure. The 9-1-1 operator says the police are already at the house."

"Can we go see?" interrupted Collin.

"No. The operator told me to wait here. Let's just wait to hear what she says."

The operator came back on the line. "*Mrs. Mitchell?*"

"Yes? I'm still here."

"*Apparently, your daughter called the police about a half hour ago, claiming she received a strange call from you and wanted the police to check out your house.*"

"Oh, my goodness! Okay. Well, should we wait, or is it safe to go to the house?"

"The police suggested you wait until they come to you."

"Uh, okay. I'm going to hang up now."

Chapter Eighteen

Early Friday Morning

Everyone climbed down the ladder as soon as they saw lights coming toward the fort. The dogs were going crazy. Collin held Gordy. Nora latched onto Cleo's collar while Sonya did the same to Amos. They saw several lights fluttering toward them, looking like large fireflies flitting about in the rain.

The first one to break out of the dark shapes was Amy, dressed in an unidentifiable dark-colored, hooded raincoat. She focused her flashlight to the ground to avoid blinding them and ran to Nora, wrapping her arms around her while Cleo and Amos sniffed at Amy's legs. "Mom! Mom! I'm so glad you're safe!"

Before Nora had a chance to say anything, Amy rushed over to the kids and embraced both Collin and Sonya in her arms. Her voice trembled with emotion. "Are you guys all right? Are you hurt? I was so worried. The house is in shambles. I didn't know what happened to you."

The officers who had accompanied Amy were also focusing their flashlights toward the ground. However, it was so dark and rainy that with their rain gear on, they simply looked like large, black shapes. It was impossible to see their faces.

A gruff voice came from one of the officers. "Mrs.

Mitchell, I'm Officer Gary McGuire. I met you last Wednesday when Officer Luke Graham and I came to your house to investigate some suspicious activity."

"Yes, I remember you both. Little did I know I'd be seeing you again so soon."

Officer McGuire asked, "Are any of you hurt? Do we need to call an ambulance?"

Nora looked at the kids. "No. Nobody is seriously injured. Just scrapes, cuts, and lots of bruises. We'll be okay. Right kids?"

"Yeah, I'm okay," Collin confirmed. "My feet hurt, but I don't need an ambulance."

"Me either," echoed Sonya.

Officer McGuire suggested, "Why don't we go back to the house? We'll take all of you to the hospital to have your wounds looked at. After that, we'll go to police headquarters where we can get this straightened out with statements from each of you as to what took place here. I understand there was a home invasion. You'll need to stay out of the house. It's now a crime scene, and we don't want to compromise any evidence we might find."

Before they walked away from the fort, Nora remembered the revolver in her pocket, where she had replaced it after shooting at Nails and Tonto. "Officer McGuire, I must tell you I have a gun in my pocket. I used it to wound one of the intruders."

"Please hand it over to me. We'll return it to you after the investigation." He took a plastic bag from his raincoat. She removed the gun from her pocket and dropped it into the bag, butt end first. He handed it to one of the policemen standing behind him.

Then Officers McGuire and Graham walked in

front of the bedraggled former captives as they trudged back to the house. Two other officers followed in the rear. The dogs finally quieted down as they trotted beside Nora and the kids. They were probably so glad to be out of the utility room that they decided not to make too much fuss with all the policemen. This had been a very upsetting experience for them also.

When the cavalcade reached the house, Nora asked Officer McGuire, "We're very wet and cold from this heavy rain. Do you think we could go in to change?"

"Well, ma'am, I don't think that'd be wise. I know you're uncomfortable. How about if my officers bring out some towels and blankets?"

Amy inquired, "What if I go in and get them some clothes. I'll take off my raincoat and shoes on the patio so I don't get any water inside."

"I suppose that'll work. I'll send an officer in with you. Get some clothing and blankets and towels. They can dry off and wrap themselves in the blankets until we get to the hospital." He turned to look at Nora. "Then all of you can change there."

Amy removed her coat and shoes and slipped on gloves and booties that one of the cops had given her. The drenched and shivering foursome waited outside on the covered patio while Amy opened the door to the screened porch. Nora remarked before Amy entered the house, "Grab something for Deet too. And shoes for Sonya and Collin."

Amy looked back rather strangely at her mother, but said, "Okay."

After several minutes, Amy brought out a plastic bag full of clothing. The officer who had accompanied her handed out towels and blankets to the shivering quartet. After they dried off, they each wrapped a blanket around themselves and headed for the police vehicles. The rain was finally slowing to a heavy drizzle.

When they walked around to the front of the house, the first thing Nora noticed was the absence of the black van belonging to the criminals. It gave her the answer to whether or not those hoodlums were in custody. They'd escaped before the police arrived.

Sonya and Nora were directed to the patrol car with Officers McGuire and Graham. Deet and Collin were put in another police car with two other officers. Amy followed in her car. Four other law enforcers remained at the house. Nora didn't think Smith Township had that many individuals on their police force. Perhaps some were from surrounding areas, like Sebring or Beloit. Maybe even Mahoning County Sheriff Department. As she looked back at the house when the cruiser pulled away, the lights inside and out were ablaze.

At the hospital, the drenched group first changed into dry clothing before being checked for injuries. Shedding her soaked garments helped to calm Nora's emotions. She was x-rayed but had no broken bones. The rosy-purple-gray bruises on her face, arms, and side were treated and bandaged. The nurse put drops into the injured eye.

Since Deet had no injuries, after he changed into one of Collin's T-shirts and a pair of his shorts, he was told to sit in the waiting area with one of the officers. The police had contacted his parents and requested they meet him at the police station.

Nora joined him to wait for Amy and the kids.

When they came out, Sonya proclaimed to Nora, "I feel so much better now." Both she and Collin also had bandages over several parts of their bodies.

"I know what you mean, honey. I do, too. It kind of feels like something dirty and contaminated has been removed."

Sonya had a pensive look on her face. "Yeah, you're right. It does."

Nora asked both the kids, "How about your feet? How bad are they?"

Collin answered for the two of them, "They don't feel too bad now. The nurse cleaned them and put some kind of medicine on them. Then she bandaged both our feet. She told us to keep the bandages on for at least two days. She also gave us some kind of cream to put on them until they healed all the way."

"Yeah, and she gave Mom a prescription to get filled. Some kind of antibiotic," added Sonya.

"Good. I was worried they might get infected."

They left the hospital with gauze, ointments, white wraps, and Band-Aids on many of their body parts. Nora also was given a script for antibiotics. Then the police escorted them to the station in the same cop vehicles in which they had ridden to the hospital. When they arrived, a different officer escorted each of them to separate, small conference rooms.

Officer McGuire explained to Nora that they wanted to isolate them to hear each individual account of their experience. Amy requested to be present in the rooms with both Sonya and Collin when they gave their testimonies. Thus, Collin waited with another officer while Amy first went in the room with Sonya.

Nora was led into an area with drab gray walls and

a square, somewhat battered, metal table in the corner. Two heavy, metal chairs were on opposite sides of the table. Detective Theresa Capella sat on the opposite side. Nora's chair scraped against the cement floor as she moved it closer to the table to rest her arms. Detective Capella asked, "Mrs. Mitchell, I want you to tell me what happened in your house these last few days. Do you mind if I record your account? I also may ask you questions after you give me your statement."

Nora agreed to her recording the session and then told her everything, starting with her experience Tuesday night when the thugs harassed her on the way home from picking up the pizza from Zep's. She mentioned the broken doggie door on the sun porch and the flicker of light she briefly saw in the woods that night. She told the officer the shape of the boy's fort where she suspected some vagrant had smoked cigarettes and drank beer, maybe more than one intruder because more than one cigarette and one beer can were found. Then she told her about Deet coming to the house so late with the men forcing their way inside. Finally, she recapped her experience being held prisoner for those few days.

Detective Capella took notes while Nora gave her statement. On completing it, the officer asked several questions. "You said you didn't know or recognize the perpetrators. Could you describe them?"

"Well, all three were tall and muscular, about six feet or more. Tomas Ramirez, who they called Tonto, was the shortest and a little paunchy around the waist. He has straight, black hair, kind of long, greasy, and combed back behind his ears. He didn't have much of a beard when we first saw his face. His skin is a deep bronze, and his eyes are beady black with heavy eyebrows. You probably already know he's Deet's uncle.

"Nails, whose real name is Bobby, probably Robert, Naylor, has mousy-brown hair, tawny skin. He was unshaven when we first saw him but not a huge beard. He has deep-set, hazel eyes, and his nose is wide and crooked, maybe broken once.

"Then there's Primo, Mr. Alan Priestley, a very evil man. I swear his demonic traits pervade his very being. And his bad breath was enough to knock you over. He has sandy-colored hair, a long nose, and a square-like, prominent chin that juts forward."

After her descriptions, she glanced at her hands on the table and shook her head.

"They were three vile creatures."

Officer Capella scanned her notes. "You mentioned the assailants were also injured. How so?"

"Well, as I said, I shot Alan Priestley in his right shoulder when we were in my husband's office. He was bleeding pretty badly when the kids and I escaped. As for the other two, not sure if they had any serious injuries. Sonya did put a long scratch on Bobby Naylor's right cheek. It bled quite a bit, might even leave a scar." She paused, remembering what happened after she shot at Tonto and Nails and thinking about one of the most important aspects aiding in their escape.

"Oh, Nails and Tonto must've sustained some other injuries because Sonya and Collin really hammered them with the baseball bat and an iron bar. I don't know if they have any serious injuries since we got out of the house as fast as possible after the kids and the dogs escaped." She grinned when she gave the detective that information.

Officer Cappella looked at her notes again. "You mentioned they took all the valuables from the house and probably what was in your safe. Could you give me an estimate on what all that was worth?"

Nora twisted her lips and shook her head, trying to come up with an answer. "Oh, my gosh. I don't know. Hundreds of thousands of dollars. The jewelry alone was worth over a hundred grand. And the cash in the safe was close to fifty or hundred. And the stocks…"

She hesitated, trying to come up with a ballpark number. "That reminds me. I must get in touch with my broker as soon as possible to halt any payouts on my stocks and bonds."

"You can do that as soon as we're done here. Those criminals won't be able to get anything from those immediately."

Nora breathed a sigh. "Oh, good."

Detective Capella sympathetically glanced at her. "Mrs. Mitchell, I know this is hard for you. You and your grandchildren went through a terrible ordeal. We're going to catch these guys. Knowing their names is a definite plus in finding them."

Nora shuddered as she sniffled and wiped tears from her eyes with her knuckle. "You know, they were going to kill us, right? Why else would Primo have given us their names? It was bad enough for them when Sonya tore off Nails' mask. But when Primo exposed both Tonto and his own faces and then their actual identity, I knew from that moment on, I had to get us out of there before he killed us."

Detective Capella turned around and grabbed a box of tissues from a shelf behind her. She handed the box to Nora. "I know this has been a life changing, horrible experience." She leaned across the table toward Nora with her elbows supporting her. As Nora continued to wipe away her tears, the officer promised, "Mark my word. We'll get these bastards."

The detective stood up, signifying she was done with her interview. Then she announced, "One last thing; we're going to need a list of all that was stolen from your house and your best guess on its value. I know that may be difficult but do the best you can. The more you remember, the better chance of our retrieving your property and getting it back to you."

Nora stood also and pocketed the used tissues. "Thank you so much for your empathy. I'm so grateful for all the police have done."

"No. Thank you. You've been very helpful and extremely brave. We appreciate your cooperation. We'll give you a few days to complete your list."

The detective went to the door and opened it for Nora. "Oh, another thing. Your home is a crime scene now. Is there any place you can stay for a few days while the CSI unit does their work?"

Nora stopped advancing toward the door and looked at the floor. "I suppose I can find a place, but what about my dogs? I have three of them at the house now."

"We've placed them in a kennel so they won't be in the way of the investigation. Only be for a few days."

The dogs wouldn't be very happy in a strange kennel. Dave and Nora always had someone come to the house to care for them when they went away. Depending on where they were going, oftentimes, they'd take the dogs with them. If they left them home, sometimes Amy and the kids cared for them. Nora hired the Pembertons' son a few times. The dogs were used to the boy and never gave him any problems. But she was sure a couple of days in some lodging would be okay. If they could withstand being in that utility room for two straight days living in piss and shit, they'd be able to survive a nice kennel for a short while.

Officer Capella asked, "By the way, what are the names of the dogs? I'd like to inform the kennel."

"The black Lab is Amos; the Doberman is Cleo; and the Pomeranian is Gordy. Oh, I have a request. Could you ask the kennel to keep the three of them in the same enclosure? They're so used to each other. They'll be more comfortable together."

The detective agreed to make sure her request was followed, and Nora went out to the common area to await Amy and the kids.

Chapter Nineteen

Friday Morning

Sonya had completed her interview and was in the waiting area when Nora finished her session with Officer Capella. Nora sat beside her granddaughter who was staring despondently into space. Nora queried, "Are you okay, honey?"

"Yeah, I'm okay. I'm just a little tired."

"No wonder. We haven't had any decent sleep since this ordeal began."

She put her arm around Sonya. "Are you sure you're okay, about this whole, crazy nightmare?"

Sonya turned to her grandmother. "Seriously, Granny, I'm okay. Yeah, it was terrible. No doubt, at times I was really scared. I didn't know if they were gonna kill us or maybe rape us." She gave Nora a glint of a sly smile. "But we did it, didn't we? We got away. We got away from three big guys with guns. You, me, and Collin. Two kids and a grandma. We did it."

Nora hugged her closer. "Yes, we did, sweetheart. We sure did."

The two of them sat quietly for a while. Both of them were regurgitating that nightmare, going over the alarming events in their heads. Finally, Nora asked Sonya something she had wondered about. "Honey, how did you get loose from the duct tape, you and

Collin, without Nails and Tonto seeing you?"

This time Sonya gave her a wider smile. "You know, it wasn't as hard as we thought it would be. We just kept wiggling and twisting our wrists, hitting them against the back of the chair. That edge really helped. We moved our feet back and forth and side by side, also bumping them against the chair legs. Most of the time, Tonto and Nails were dozing, so they didn't pay any attention to us. Deet wanted to come over to help, but he was afraid if he got out of his chair, they'd wake up. So we just kept up the twisting and kicking. I felt my hands break free first, but I knew I couldn't move them from the tape to release my feet. That would be too noticeable. So I just held my hands close together and worked on getting my feet loose."

"That's amazing." Her grandmother kissed her on the cheek. "And to think the two of you were able to get those weapons just in time. I couldn't believe it when I saw you come in behind Tonto and Nails and start bashing them. Those men were just about to shoot me."

"Yeah, I didn't know if I could do it. Neither did Collin. But we talked about it after you left with Primo to open the safe and decided we *had* to do it. Then when we heard the gun shot and Nails and Tonto rushed into the office, we didn't even think about it. We took the tape off our feet, and the tape was still hanging from our hands. I ran to the kitchen for the pipe. Collin got the baseball bat, releasing the dogs at the same time. When we reached the office doorway, we saw Nails raise his gun to shoot at you, so we couldn't waste a second. We caught them off guard when we started pounding on them until you ran past us. We didn't even think. We just did it."

"Well, you two saved my life, you know." She hugged her again.

"Granny, you saved all of our lives. Even Deet. They were gonna kill him too. I heard them whispering about it. Primo didn't trust him. Tonto tried to change Primo's mind, but in the end he gave in and agreed to it. I couldn't believe it. His own nephew!"

Nora agreed with Sonya. How could an uncle kill his own flesh and blood? What madmen. "Deet is just a mixed-up kid. I hope this tragedy helps him see that more clearly, and he gets some help."

"I think he's gonna talk to his dad about all this. His dad is not like Tonto. He's a good guy. He works hard for the family at some warehouse. His mom too. She's a waitress at a Mexican restaurant on Mahoning Avenue. They're good people. Kyle and I have been trying to convince Deet to leave that weed alone and stop drinking. I thought he was listening. Maybe he will now. After all, he's gonna have to come clean to his dad how he got involved in all this."

Nora shook her head. "And to the authorities too. He'll have to pay for what he did even if he is a kid."

Collin and Amy came walking down the hall from the conference area followed by another detective. Collin was wiping his eyes with his forearm. Nora got out of her seat and went to him. "Are you okay, sweetheart?"

"Yeah, I'm okay. That was just hard. It was like it was happening all over again. But I'm okay now."

"Collin, I'm so proud of you and your sister. Nobody could've done any better. Had it not been for you and her, they would've killed all of us." She hugged him tightly, then turned to Amy. "These are very special kids you have, Amy."

"Mom, I know that. And you are a very special mother." Then they held each other, both crying. Sonya and Collin joined them in a heartfelt group hug.

A few minutes later, the police chief came over to Nora and asked if she and the kids could wait around the station for a little while longer in case the detectives had any additional questions. While they waited, Amy and Nora talked about the incident and its effect on everyone. "Mom, I cried both times when the kids gave their statements. I'm so proud of them."

"Amy, these kids were amazing. I wish they hadn't been there with me so they wouldn't have had to experience that terrifying torment. To tell the truth, if it wasn't for them, I know I wouldn't have survived. I'm sure if I hadn't lost those thugs Tuesday night coming home from Zep's in my minivan, we'd all be dead."

They probably hugged each other again for a full two minutes after that statement.

Nora also used the time waiting to question Amy about their rescue. "How was it the police were at the house before my call to 9-1-1? I was shocked when the operator told me the police had already arrived."

"Don't you remember? You hinted to me in the phone call we had that everything was not right. You said Lisa was so anxious for your visit. Mom, she never said that; you'd never expect her to say it. I knew something was wrong. After the funeral, you were so adamant about not wanting to go to Brian's house. At first, I was confused, and it took me a while to figure it out. But finally, last night in bed, I couldn't sleep. I started thinking about our conversation, and I realized you were actually sending me a message indicating things were not okay. I called the police right away. I'm sorry I didn't catch on to the hint sooner. Maybe if the police had arrived earlier, they could've caught the intruders."

Nora had a different opinion. "You know, I think it's probably better it happened the way it did, and you called when you did. Suppose the police confronted those monsters either from inside or outside the house while we were still bound to our chairs in the living room. Most likely, there would've been a hostage situation. Those demons had their guns in their hands at all times. If they felt threatened, they may have killed all of us without blinking an eye and ended up battling it out with the police, who might've been killed or hurt too. I think it was better the way it went down, even if they weren't caught—yet. And the kids and I escaped with only minor injuries."

"You're right. It could've been much worse. I'm just so sorry you and the kids had to endure all that."

While they sat at the station, Amy called Carlos, the kids' father. Twenty minutes later, he came rushing into the front door, his eyes like saucers, looking around for his children, his mother Mercedes following him with the same look of concern. When the kids saw him, they ran to him, hugging, talking, and crying all at the same time. Amy and Nora stood, waiting for Carlos to come over to them. He approached them with each arm wrapped around one of the children. Mercedes had her arm around Sonya also.

Carlos first addressed Nora. "Mama Mitchell, I am so sorry." He released the kids and deeply hugged her.

"Thank you, Carlos. I'm okay now."

He held her at arms' length, and then clutched her

hand. "You are a strong woman, Mama."

"Well, I tell you. If it wasn't for those wonderful kids of yours, the three of us wouldn't be here to talk about it."

He nodded his head. "Yes, yes. They are very special." Then he dropped her hands and approached Amy. Mercedes came to Nora and also hugged her.

When Carlos came up to Amy, she had a look of hesitation in her expression, but as he reached out to hug her, she responded. They embraced each other for a full minute. Nora didn't know when they had last spoken to one another face to face.

As Amy and Carlos released their embrace, Deet and his parents came down the hall from the conference area. Nora quickly skirted over to them. "Mr. and Mrs. Ramirez, whatever happens, your son helped us escape. He's a good boy. He just needs to start listening to the right people."

Woefully, Mr. Ramirez responded, "Thank you, ma'am. We don't know yet how they will charge Diego in your kidnapping. I know my brother, that son of a bitch, was very involved. I am so sorry for his actions."

"No. No. You don't have to apologize for your brother. You are not he. Just take care of Deet, I mean Diego. If there's anything I can do, please let me know."

"That is very kind of you."

Nora went to Deet. He didn't want to look at her. She touched his chin and gently lifted it. "Deet? I'm not angry with you. We are all safe. But let this be a lesson for you to start listening to your parents and not your uncle or anyone else who would steer you in the wrong direction."

She gave him a hug. "Take care, young man."

As Deet and his family left the building, Sonya raised her hand slightly and waved to him. Nora hoped he would mend his ways before he turned out like his uncle.

They were free to go. Go where? Nora couldn't go home. Since her phone wasn't charged, she asked Amy what time it was. Amy looked at her phone. "It's twenty till nine"

"Oh, my gosh! The kids must be beat—and starving."

She was tired and hungry too. "Hey kids, you two must be very sleepy. Do you want to go home or get something to eat first?"

They opted to take care of the hunger before nap time. Carlos and his mom joined them as they started off to get breakfast. Collin and Sonya rode with Carlos to the restaurant. Nora rode with Amy. This was the first chance mother and daughter had to talk alone since—well, Nora wasn't quite sure. It must have been before Dave's funeral. All their recent phone calls had been monitored by Primo. Also, since the police had found them, it had been a whirlwind of questions, answers, tears, and hugs.

Amy started the car and fretted. "Mom, are you really okay?"

"I guess it takes a near death experience to wake a person up and realize that no matter what has been thrown your way, life is precious and worth living. And fighting for."

While driving, Amy briefly glanced at her mother and placed her hand on her shoulder. "I was definitely worried about you after Dad's funeral. You were so sad and depressed. But who wouldn't be? We all were mourning his loss."

"I was worried myself. I didn't feel like living anymore. The first good thing was for you to insist the kids stay with me for a while. They forced me to keep my mind off my own tragedy and focus on them. Then this horrible nightmare happened. Well, there wasn't much time during the last few days to mourn your dad's death or to feel sorry for myself. I spent every moment either putting up with the abuse from those kidnappers or trying to figure a way to escape and save our lives."

Amy glanced at her again. "I listened to both Sonya and Collin's account of what happened. No wonder they were terrified. But I'm proud of the three of you. You were all so amazing and brave."

Nora closed her eyes briefly, remembering some of the horror. "It undoubtedly was an experience we will never forget but never want to live through again."

"Mom, what about the bank? The kids said you left yesterday morning to get money out of the bank?"

Nora exhaled a deep sigh. "Oh, yeah. I knew that wasn't going to work out, but I had to waste time until I thought of some way to gain our freedom. The bank said I'd have to wait four to seven days to get my money. I can't even imagine being with those bastards a minute longer than what we were. None of us, even those thieves, could've lasted one more day." She shuddered. "Horrible, horrible!"

Amy pulled into the parking lot at the restaurant. Carlos' car was already there with the kids getting out of the car doors. In the restaurant, they sat at a large booth. Nora was surprised to see Carlos sitting next to Amy.

Nora and the kids were starving. They had to forego dinner the night before in order to carry out their escape plan. Therefore, they hadn't eaten since lunch yesterday. And it was way past their breakfast time.

While they ate, Amy asked, "So, Mom, since you can't go home yet, are you coming back to my apartment?"

Nora actually hadn't had a chance to think about where she'd go, with everything else going on. "I don't know right now. I suppose I will, at least for today. Then I'm not sure."

Amy seemed hesitant to add to her question. "Can I make a suggestion?"

Nora's fork was in her hand with a bite of potatoes on it. "Of course, you can."

"I see that you have two easy options. I'm sure you know the first one. You can stay with us at the apartment as long as you want."

Nora put the chunk of potatoes in her mouth and chewed while waiting for Amy's next suggestion.

"Or, better yet, you can spend some time at Brian and Lisa's house."

She barely finished her statement when Nora reacted. "Amy, you know Lisa doesn't like me. If I stayed there, she'd hate me by the time I left."

Amy argued, "Mom, you really never gave her a chance. I agree, both Brian and Lisa can be a little pompous at times. But this is a chance for you to talk about some of the issues you have with them."

Nora put her fork down and shook her head. "Oh, that would be great. Spending my time arguing with two bullheaded, highfaluting egotists. I love Brian dearly, but I know if I spend more than an hour with him, I'll want to kill him. Your dad was always the mediator when Brian was around. Going there would probably put me back into a depression."

"Oh, come on. It can't be that bad."

"Amy, think back when you were kids. Did you ever get along with your brother?"

Without hesitation, Amy pronounced, "Yeah, I did. I'm not saying we had a great sibling relationship. We were six years apart, and he was a boy. We didn't have much in common, and we didn't have the same friends. But we weren't at each other's throats constantly. Face it, Mom. You don't get along with him because you two are just alike. Pigheaded and unforgiving. And actually, he has mellowed since Marcus was born."

"What do you mean? I don't put on airs like he does, thinking I'm the smartest, most influential, perfect person on this planet."

"Oh, he really doesn't act like that. Neither do you." She leaned forward and put her elbows on the table. "When was the last time you actually spent time with him? Like just the two of you. I bet it's been years. You don't really know him now. I admit Lisa can be a little, well, condescending at times. But underneath that exterior, she has a good heart. You have to remember she came from money. She's never had to struggle to achieve anything in life. But if you talk to her, really talk to her, you'll find she's more understanding than you'd think. You need to give them both a chance."

Nora began eating again, swirling the things Amy had said in her mind while stabbing at her eggs. Everyone else in the booth had been quiet during their discussion/disagreement. Carlos and Mercedes seemed uncomfortable. Collin was busy stuffing his face, oblivious to the conversation.

But Sonya kept looking back and forth between her mother and grandmother. She finally focused on Nora when there was a lull in the argument. "You know, Granny, I think it'd be fun to stay at Uncle Brian's house. We've never done that before. There's so much more to do around his place, like the beach and the amusement park. I was really young when we visited him the last time. I'd love to see their house. I don't remember much about it, but Mom says it's gorgeous. What if Collin and I go with you for a while? It doesn't have to be for a long visit, just until the police let you go home. Then we can go back with you to your house for the rest of the summer."

At first, Nora didn't say anything. She was surprised with the idea. Sonya smiled at her. "Maybe Collin and I could be the referees in case you and Aunt Lisa start punching each other."

She definitely broke the ice with that statement. Everyone chuckled, and Nora muttered, "Okay, okay. I'll think about it."

Chapter Twenty

Friday Evening

After breakfast everyone went to Amy's apartment. Nora was so tired she felt like she was sleepwalking, and she immediately lay down on Amy's bed. The kids didn't take naps right away. Before Nora fell asleep, she heard conversations coming from the living room. It was good for them to talk to their mom and dad about how they had dealt with the turmoil of the last few days. Nora took pleasure in knowing they were not holding everything inside.

When she woke up from her nap, she looked at the clock on the bedside table. Six-thirty in the evening. Would she be able to sleep at bedtime? She felt refreshed but still a little groggy. She got up, used the restroom, and went into the living room.

The apartment had an open floor plan. Mercedes was watching a Spanish channel on the television. Carlos and Amy sat at the kitchen table deep in an intimate conversation. The kids were asleep in their bedrooms. Nora didn't want to interrupt the kitchen discussion, so she sat on the couch next to Mercedes, where she casually glanced at the television, Mercedes smiled at her and handed her the remote. Nora objected, "Oh no. You watch what you want. I'm just waking up." Mercedes nodded her head, kept the remote, and continued watching her program.

The couple in the kitchen noticed Nora had awakened. Amy suggested, "Mom, you're up? Do you want a cup of coffee?"

"I'd love one."

Their private chat had obviously come to an end. Getting off the couch, she joined them in the kitchen. "That sounds perfect." Amy always made good coffee. It was already brewed in her pot. Nora helped herself to a mug from the cupboard, poured the coffee, and sat at the table with Carlos and Amy.

Carlos commented, "I hope you had a nice nap, Mama."

"No dreaming. No nightmares. Just precious sleep. Maybe too much. I probably won't sleep tonight."

Nora took a few sips of her coffee. "This is exactly what I need right now."

Amy stared into her own coffee mug. Without looking at her mother, she revealed, "Mom, I called Brian." Then she glanced in Nora's direction. "He was a little upset you hadn't called him yourself."

Any small talk was apparently over. Nora continued drinking her coffee and didn't respond to Amy's subtle accusation.

"Come on, Mom. You know you're being childish. Even Sonya noticed it. He's your son, for goodness sakes!"

Another sip of the black liquid. "You're right. I should've called him. I have no excuse."

"Why don't you call him now?"

Nora glanced at the kitchen clock. "They're probably having dinner. Lisa doesn't like to be disturbed at dinnertime."

Amy raised her voice. "Oh, cut it out. This is not just a social call. Brian needs to know you're okay. He needs to hear it from you. This is getting ridiculous. You can be so loving and concerned for me and the kids, but it's like you're a different person with Brian." She stared at her. "Why is that? I don't understand."

Nora knew she was right. She didn't understand it either, but she had to fix it. Amy was right about Lisa too. Nora never even tried to get to know or understand the woman. No time like the present to get started.

She put down her coffee mug and stood up. "Can I use your cellphone? I haven't had a chance to charge mine yet."

Amy quickly reached in her pocket and handed her mother the phone. "Gladly. Here it is." She smiled as she handed it to her.

Nora went back into the bedroom, sat on the bed, and pressed Brian's number.

"Hey, Amy, what's up? Is Mom okay?"

"Brian, it's Mom."

His voice sounded very concerned. *"Oh, Mom, why didn't you call me? Are you okay? Amy told me about the kidnappers. What can I do? Do you want me to come over?*

"You don't have to come here. Everything is okay now. I'm sorry I didn't call you sooner."

"Oh, I understand. You had more important things to think about. Are you sure you're okay? Amy said they shot at you. Oh my God! Mom, that had to be so frightening."

"Yes, it was. I'm just so glad it's over and the kids and I survived."

"Have the thieves been apprehended?"

"I don't know. I haven't heard anything from the police yet. Did Amy tell you we saw their faces and know their names?"

"Oh, my God. No, she didn't mention that. That'll make it so much easier for the police to catch them."

"I hope so." She paused to get up the nerve to ask him the question she needed to ask. "Brian, I can't get into my house for a couple of days and—" She didn't get to finish her request.

"Why don't you come stay with Lisa and me? We'd love to have you. I'll take a few days off work. It's been so long since we've spent time together."

"Actually, that was what I had in mind to ask you. I thought it'd give me a chance to get to know Lisa a little better. I know I'm not her favorite person."

"That's not true. She really does like you. She just thinks you don't like her. You two need to talk this out."

"You're right, son. I'm looking forward to sitting down with her *and* you."

Nora was silent for a few seconds.

"Mom? Are you still there?"

"Yes, I'm still here. There's something else."

"What is it?"

Her voice cracked with emotion. "Brian, I need to apologize to you for the way I've acted in the past. I love you, son. I hope you know that." She couldn't help it. Tears rolled down her cheeks.

"I know, Mom. I love you too. You have nothing to apologize for."

"Well, I haven't always been as kind to you and Lisa as I should've been. You know that."

"No. No, I don't. It's just that we haven't been as close as we should be, what with not living near each

218

other, our jobs, and everything else. We're going to fix that with this visit. Right?"

He was just being kind. She knew he felt the animosity over the years, and she was so, so sorry for it. She had to tell him that. She was the parent here. She should've known better. "You are too much of a gentleman to admit that your mother is a bossy, abrasive old broad. But that's all going to change, Brian." She sobbed more heavily. "You're absolutely right. We're going to fix all of it."

"No, no. That's not true. Don't say those things, Mom. We may have had our differences, but you've been a good mother." His voice got emotional too as he offered, *"Do you want me to come and get you tomorrow?"*

She grabbed a tissue from Amy's bedside table and dabbed her eyes. "Uh, no, I think I'll drive out there in the morning after I pick up some clothes from my house." She remembered about the kids. "Uh, Brian, is it okay if Sonya and Collin come with me? They were staying at my house for the summer; they were there when the men broke in the house."

"Yes, Amy told me. I'd like to hear all about it from the three of you. Please bring the kids with you. We'd love to have them. too."

After saying their goodbyes and expressing her deep love for Brian, Nora hung up. She felt so much better, finally realizing she had been petty and unreasonable for way too long. Like Amy said, and she agreed, she could really be a bitch at times.

She went back into the kitchen with a smile on her face and handed Amy her phone. With eyes wide open, Amy tilted her head and looked at her mother, waiting for her to speak. Nora didn't make her wait. "I'm driving over to Brian's tomorrow with the kids."

Amy jumped out of her chair and gave her mother a big hug. "Thank you, Mom! Thank you!"

Chapter Twenty-One

Saturday Morning

On Friday night, since Nora didn't know if she'd be able to sleep after such a long nap earlier, she insisted Amy sleep in her own bed while Nora took the couch. Actually, she did get more rest despite the nap. She woke up about five-thirty and made coffee. It wasn't long before the others awakened.

Nora had discussed with the kids the night before that they'd be going to Brian's house for a few days. Both Sonya and Collin were all for it. At eight she called the police station to see how she could get some of her clothes to take to Brian's. They told her Officer McGuire would meet her at the house at ten. Amy would drive her so Nora could pick up her car. Carlos was taking the kids to spend a few hours with them before she took them to Hunting Valley.

Nora was curious about the way Amy and Carlos were acting lately. She brought up her interest on the ride to her house. "Amy, not that it's any of my business, but what's going on with you and Carlos?"

Amy acted coy. "What do you mean?"

"Well, the two of you seem to be having some cozy conversations lately."

Amy didn't respond, but Nora didn't let it go. "Am I right?"

After a few seconds, while looking out the front windshield and not at her mother, Amy blurted, "Carlos wants to get back together again."

It took Nora by surprise. "You're kidding."

"No, I'm not."

"How do you feel about that? You two have been divorced for quite a few years."

Amy briefly looked over toward Nora, her voice filled with emotion. "I've thought about it at times. But if it doesn't work out, the kids will be heartbroken. I can't do that to them again."

Nora surmised something like that was going on. Neither of them spoke for a couple of minutes. She waited in case Amy had more to say.

She did. This time, with concern in her voice, Amy questioned, "What do you think?"

"Hey, this is your life. I can't make that decision for you." She wanted to say more but didn't want to influence Amy's judgement. She did offer, "I agree with your apprehension because of the kids. If you do it, it has to be for keeps. At least until they're not children any longer. It would devastate them if the two of you broke up a second time."

"I know. That's the problem. That's why Carlos and I have to be sure it'll work the second time around."

Nora had to ask her the most important question. "Do you still love Carlos?"

Amy turned to her with a doleful smile. "I never stopped loving him."

"Then what *is* the problem here?"

Amy kept driving, trying to put her feelings into words. "It's just that, well, it didn't work out the first time, and there's no guarantee it'd be different the second time."

"Hey, I agree. I've certainly learned that life has no guarantees. Sure, it didn't work out the first time for you, but remember, the two of you were in a different place in your lives. You need to be aware of this. There's never any assurance about most everything. There's no recipe or map to follow to guarantee you'll have a happy life. However, one thing you both have going for you now is that you're older and more mature. You were both kids when you got married. You had a lot to learn. You were thrust into adulthood before you had a chance to plan for it or experience many of the things that help kids grow up. Your dad and I tried to help, but in the end, it was up to the two of you."

"That's what I'm thinking too. And Carlos agrees."

As adults, daughters don't always discuss their sex lives with their mothers. Hell, as teenagers they don't either. When Amy had gotten pregnant with Sonya, it wasn't until she started to actually show that Nora became aware of the pregnancy. Thus, she wasn't sure if her daughter would open up to her now. But she was inquisitive about this aspect of both Carlos and Amy's lives. "Have either of you had any serious relationships since the divorce?"

"Not me. I dated a couple of guys, just casually. I was too busy starting my career and taking care of the kids. Sure, Carlos was good about paying child support. Of course, the government automatically deducted it from his pay, but he never complained to me and definitely not to the kids. It's just that he wasn't there to help me with the emotional and physical things I needed. So I became independent, not counting on anyone else. And that's my issue now. Would I resent him for making decisions I'm used to handling on my own? And do I want to give up that independence?

Her words hit home for Nora. "That's just the opposite of what I'll need to deal with now with your dad gone. Depending on someone is good, but what it comes down to is that you have to be able to go it alone. I found that out this week. So I'm facing what you had to face years ago. You learned how to do it, and you've done a great job with it."

"I hope you're right. Do you think I can go back now?"

"I don't think you really have to go back at all. The two of you are definitely different people now than when you first met. And you're both in a different phase of your lives from fifteen years ago. You both know where your lives are headed career wise. In that respect, you're both established. Even though neither of you are rich, you each have made a decent living. So money won't be as much of an issue this time around like last time."

Silence again. Then Amy spoke. "You know, Carlos was an alcoholic."

Nora patted her on her shoulder. "I suspected something like that when the two of you were going through your most difficult times. You never said anything then, but your dad and I talked about it and decided it was between you and Carlos. We assumed if you wanted to discuss it with us, you would do so. When you didn't, we didn't want to interfere. Maybe we should've been more forthcoming."

Nora paused then asked, "How is he now? Do you

know if he's still drinking?"

Immediately, Amy pointed out, "Oh, he hasn't had a drink in three years. Sonya knew about his problem. She said when they'd visit him before, he always smelled of booze, and he acted what she called 'weird', but she says it's been a long time since she's seen that behavior. She said he's very different now on their visits. He hangs out with them, cooks for them, and they enjoy spending time with him."

"I'm so glad to hear that. It's important whether or not the two of you get back together that they too are on board with it."

Amy was quiet again. A few minutes passed. Then she revealed, "Carlos had one serious girlfriend about a year after the divorce."

"Oh. Did he tell you about it?"

"Well, at first Sonya told me. You know Sonya; nothing gets by her. Then I asked him about it. I felt I had the right to know who was in my kids' lives. She was living with him for a while, so she would naturally be interacting with them."

"Do you know what happened to that relationship?"

"Not really. I think they lived together for about six months. Out of the blue, one day Sonya said, 'I'm glad Rosa doesn't live with Daddy anymore.' And that was that. Carlos never mentioned her again, and I didn't either. If she was gone from his apartment, it was really none of my business any longer. As far as I know, she was the only serious relationship he had. I'm sure Sonya would've mentioned it if he had any others. She's very observant, and sometimes she tells me things she probably shouldn't."

"Yeah, she's something else, that girl."

Nora brought up another point with Amy that she thought was important. "One thing you do need to think about." She touched her shoulder again. "The kids aren't going to be with you forever. Soon they'll have their own lives to live. It'll seem to happen so quickly. You'll always be their mother, but eventually you'll take second place to their spouses and their own children. And that's the way it should be. You try to raise them to be independent and self-sufficient. But when they are on their own, you'll be alone. Is that something you want to look forward to? Everybody's different. Some people are happy on their own. They like the freedom that comes from not dealing with another human continually—their bad habits, their peculiarities, their faults. Then there are others who need a partner, someone by their side to help them cope with the negative aspects of life and share with them the positive parts—no matter what bad characteristics they have. Maybe you should think about what type of a person you are. Would you want to be alone for the rest of your life? If not, is Carlos the one with whom you'd like to spend those years?"

"You're right, Mom. I guess I do need to think about that." She waited a few seconds. "I guess Carlos needs to think about it too."

They approached Nora's house, and all conversation came to an end. Amy pulled into the driveway behind Officer McGuire's patrol car. The officer was waiting for them outside his vehicle.

Nora hadn't heard anything from the police or the news about those assholes who had held her and the kids hostage. When she and Amy got out of the car,

Nora asked Officer McGuire, "Has there been any news on Priestley and the others?"

"I'm sorry, ma'am not yet. We checked all the local hospitals for gunshot victims. Negative there, but Priestley has a long history of crime and violence. He might know someone outside the normal medical channels who could mend his wound. From what was on your office carpet, it was evident he lost a lot of blood. I'm sure he's very weak now. There was also blood in the doorway of the office. Those kids must've done some damage with their weapons to the other perpetrators too.

"My thought is that they're lying low somewhere until their wounds heal a little. We've also checked pawn shops around the area. None of your things have shown up in any of them. And the word is out to our confidential informants, although we haven't heard anything from them either.

"We checked with the families of the accused. Priestley is not married and has no significant other. His parents are dead. He has a brother Nick Priestley, who lives in California. The LAPD is checking to see if Nick has been in touch with Alan or has any knowledge of his whereabouts. Naylor's girlfriend claims she hasn't heard from him in a couple of weeks, but we're keeping our eyes on her. She's already on probation for a felony she committed, so her word might not be too reliable.

"There's a chance Tomas Ramirez might try to flee to Mexico, where his parents still live. We're watching for this also. Juan Ramirez is very upset his brother would be involved in holding you hostage and in including Diego in his criminal activities. I think he'll let us know if Tomas contacts him.

"That's about it on the offenders. The CSI crew are still working inside the house. They should be done by Monday. I'll give you a call. In the meantime, I guess you want to get some of your clothes."

"Yes, and the kids' clothes too. I'm going to stay at my son's house in Hunting Valley for a few days."

Officer McGuire nodded his head. "Good. Glad you're putting some distance between you and the crime scene."

Suddenly, Nora remembered the dogs. How could she have forgotten about her dear companions? "Oh, by the way, where were my dogs taken? Are they okay?"

"The dogs are fine. They're at the Pet Paws Hotel on Hammond Street in Youngstown. I told the owner you'd get in touch with him regarding their stay." The officer reached in his pocket. "Here's their card with their address and phone number.

"I think that about covers everything. Do you have any questions?"

"No. Not at this time." Then she remembered the list of stolen items she was supposed to prepare, which was one of the reasons she had to come back to the house. "There is something else. While I'm here, would it be okay if I compiled that list of things they stole? It'll be easier to remember if I'm able to visualize where I kept them."

"I don't see that as a problem. Just don't disturb anything in the process."

Nora and Amy were required to wear plastic gloves and foot coverings before entering the house. They stayed clear of areas where the crime crew was working or where they had marked something with tags or tape.

First, Nora retrieved one of her pieces of luggage from the attic and filled it with about a week's worth of clothes and toiletries. Amy gathered the clothes the kids had brought to their grandmother's house and put them in a couple of other suitcases. Then Nora got a pad of paper and a pen from the office, especially avoiding the blood on the carpet. She wrote down the stolen valuables from the safe. Those were the most important things on the list. She realized she'd have to call her broker on Monday to stop any illegal transactions on their stocks.

Next Nora went from room to room, looking in closets and drawers, and writing down item after item. She hadn't realized just how much those rotten bastards had taken from her. As she looked around each room, she was determined to try her best to make sure the three of them got the ultimate punishment they deserved.

Secretly, she wished she had shot and wounded all three of them. What they had done to her and her grandchildren was more costly than any of the material things they took. Those were important, but those scoundrels had taken much more—their freedom, their free will, and their dignity. No one should be stripped of those things. And had they not been stopped, they would've taken their very lives too. Nora was positive of that.

Chapter Twenty-Two

Saturday Afternoon to the Following Friday

Nora picked up the kids at their dad's apartment on her way to Hunting Valley. She had called Brian before leaving Amy's place to give him the approximate time they'd arrive. The kids were excited about staying at Brian's. On the ride, they talked about what they planned to do with their Uncle Brian and Aunt Lisa. Nora was relieved they didn't sound too traumatized from the events of the last few days. Maybe they were simply postponing their tense and disturbing feelings. Perhaps Amy might have to get some counseling for them at some point.

The three of them also sang songs on the road trip, taking turns choosing the tunes. They knew all of their grandmother's suggestions because she and Amy had often sung those to them, but she didn't know many of their choices. In fact, to Nora, most of the ones they chose didn't sound like songs at all, and each melody sounded just like the tune before it. But they enjoyed singing them. They also enjoyed her attempt at a few, especially the rap song they tried to teach her. She thought her rhythm was quite fetching. Her tongue may have gotten a little twisted, trying to talk so fast and still stay in cadence.

Nora called Brian again when they approached his

street. He and Lisa were both outside their door when the minivan pulled onto the drive.

"Wow!" gasped Collin. "I didn't remember their house being *this* big."

Sonya glanced around at the other houses on the block. "Everybody's rich on this street. These houses are bigger than yours, Granny."

"Well, I'm sure all these people have worked hard for their houses."

"Someday I want a house like one of these," admitted Collin.

"I hope you get one too, Collin. If you get a good job and work hard, there's nothing you can't do."

Brian and Lisa came down their walkway to greet them. Brian gave Nora a huge hug. She whispered in his ear, "I love you, son."

"I love you, too, Mom," he replied as he kissed her cheek.

Everybody hugged everyone before they went into the house. In the entrance hall, Collin's eyes grew wide as he admired the expansive porcelain tile floor, the shining, stark metal staircase spiraling up to the second level, the intricate original artwork adorning the walls, and the sleek, modern furnishings placed perfectly around the room.

"Wow!" Collin repeated. "You guys sure have a big house, Uncle Brian.

Brian chuckled, "Yes. I guess it is kind of big. It's so big we sometimes get lost in it."

"Really?" marveled Collin.

Brain laughed. "I'm kidding, Collin. We know our way around it by now."

Still amazed, Collin pondered, "Do you clean this

mansion every week like Mom makes us do in the apartment?"

"We have a lovely lady that comes in on Fridays to clean it thoroughly, but Lisa and I do take care of it during the rest of the week."

Then Collin frowned. "I wish Mom would hire somebody to help clean our apartment. Then *I* wouldn't have to do it."

Everyone laughed except Sonya. "Oh, Collin, don't lie. You do very little cleaning at home. Mom is lucky if you bring your dirty dishes out from your bedroom. She has to force you to clean your room."

"Well, it's hard! And I got other stuff to do."

"Like what?" sassed Sonya.

To settle the debate, Brian changed the subject. "I guess it's been a while since you've been here, Collin. How about I show you and Sonya around?"

****

Each of the kids had their own bedroom during their stay at Brian's. They did a lot of fun and entertaining things with both Brian and Lisa joining them. The kids swam in the spectacular, Olympic-size pool. They were introduced to two neighbor kids who joined them in the pool and other activities. Brian and Lisa were friends with those kids' parents. The boy, Nathan, was eleven, and the girl, Allie, was fifteen. All four kids got along great.

The group went to the beach one day and the amusement park on another. The park was a bit of a road trip, but they managed to make it seem shorter by singing and playing games along the way. At the park, they especially enjoyed the magnificent roller coasters, some of the best in the world. They also took a scenic boat ride on Lake Erie, and they fished on the lake. Everything was enjoyable and took their minds off their horrid experience from the week before.

The unexpected thing Nora did that she enjoyed the most was to see Lisa in a group of other performers doing a standup comedy routine. Yes, Lisa. See, that's how little time Nora had taken over the years to get to know her. She happened to be a very funny lady. The routine was a bit risqué, so the kids didn't join them that evening. They stayed the night at Nathan and Allie's house. Nora couldn't remember the last time she laughed so hard. The comedians were hysterical, particularly Lisa. She was the star of the show. Who would've thought? And the show was just what Nora needed to help put both Dave's death and her near death in perspective.

The night before she drove back to Smith Township, Nora had a very long talk with Brian and Lisa. She realized she really didn't even know her son at all. He wasn't the pompous asshole she accused him of being. Anything but that. He was a very caring father, loving husband, and a dedicated, compassionate man. She never imagined the charitable work he did in his community. She felt horrible about the way she'd treated him over the years.

"Brian, can you ever forgive me?"

But Brian simply fluffed it off. "Mom, there's nothing to forgive."

Seems Nora might be the only bitch in the family after all. No wonder Primo called her one so often.

She also begged Lisa for her forgiveness. She had never given herself a chance to get to know her. Had she done that like she should've years ago, she'd have discovered Lisa to be the opposite of what she had accused her of being for so long.

Officer McGuire called several times during their stay at Brian's house, keeping her abreast of the case. The crime scene unit finished with her house on Monday afternoon while they were at Brian's. She was free to return home, but they were having such a great time in Hunting Valley, they stayed until Friday afternoon.

According to Officer McGuire, the three criminals still hadn't been captured. The police brought Nails' girlfriend in for more questioning, but she consistently claimed she hadn't been in touch with Nails since before the incident. The police were keeping a look-out on social media accounts and watching her apartment in case Nails got in touch with her or showed up at her place. As frustrating as it was, Nora had to play the waiting game. It was completely out of her hands.

She and the grandkids started back toward Youngstown about two o'clock Friday afternoon. She hoped to miss the heavy traffic on Route 422.

She asked the kids, "Do you want to go home or come to my house? I need to warn you. There's a lot of nasty cleaning to do. Not just putting things back in order, but who knows what shape the office is in with me shooting Primo and the two of you pounding on Nails and Tonto?"

"I'm willing to help," volunteered Sonya.

"Me, too," added Collin. "I don't get sick when I see blood like Dad does. You wouldn't want him to help. He'd barf all over the place and pass out."

"Okay then," Nora said. "Sonya, get on your phone and find out what's the best way to clean up blood."

Sonya started searching on the internet. "It says here there are four ways to do the job: using baking soda, using salt, using liquid dish detergent, and using hydrogen peroxide. It says the best is the peroxide, but it's probably the most expensive."

"Hmm," Nora said out loud. "I guess I'll buy all of them. It won't hurt. I'll need a lot of paper towels, too."

They stopped at a superstore on their way out of Hunting Valley to purchase all the supplies. Then Nora called Amy from the car and told her their plans. Amy said she'd come out to the house that evening after work and stay the weekend.

Before she drove home, Nora also stopped at the Pet Paw Hotel to pick up the dogs. They were so excited to see her and the kids. Gordy jumped so much on her legs she had to pick him up to comfort him. He couldn't give her enough kisses. Amos and Cleo couldn't stop nuzzling against the three of them. Nora felt so much better, seeing them so happy and knowing they had been well cared for. They too had gone through a terrible nightmare. It was comforting, but crowded, having them in the minivan with them on the way to Smith Township.

When they arrived at Nora's house and as soon as they unpacked the car, they started right in with the cleaning. Although Nora knew it was impossible, she wanted to rid the place of every trace of those bastards. She started the job of cleaning up the blood in the office and the more minor amount in the living room. On her phone, she found the website Sonya had seen suggesting the best way to remove the bloodstains.

Some had splattered on the walls also. Those she washed and painted over the spots with leftover paint she had in the basement. As for the carpet, she planned to eventually replace it. However, in the meantime she and the kids worked to remove as much of the stains as possible until she bought the new carpeting. No way did she need to see that reminder every time she walked into the office.

When they had done the best they could on the carpet, Sonya took on the task of straightening up the house, putting things away, sweeping up messes, throwing out trash. Collin and Nora tried to mend the doggie door on the screen porch. They patched the broken plastic with some strips of wood. Nora planned to buy a new one at Leonard's Hardware Store, but they at least gave it a temporary fix.

The three of them had eaten a huge lunch before they left Brian's house, enabling them to work straight through with only pauses for drinks and bathroom breaks until Amy arrived at seven that evening. She stopped at Zep's and picked up a variety of delicious food. The workers were starving after their day of heavy labor.

"Thanks, Amy, for the food. I guess we didn't realize we were so hungry. Right, kids?"

They both nodded their heads, unable to speak as they munched on their calzones.

"Hey, it's the least I can do. Sorry I couldn't help with the cleanup." She gazed around the room. "Looks like you guys did a good job without me."

"Yeah, Mom," taunted Sonya. "You could've quit early and come out and helped."

"Yeah, Mom," echoed Collin. "Party pooper."

Everything in the house was back in order. Well, at least the things that were left behind by the bastards.

The police had returned Nora's revolver, the iron pipe, and the baseball bat after they had examined and done with them what they needed to do. Nora had reloaded and replaced the gun back into the panty liner box. They say lightning doesn't strike the same place twice, but she wasn't taking any chances. She wanted to remain prepared just in case it struck again at her house.

While Collin put the baseball bat in its place in the utility room, Sonya asked, "Where does the iron pipe go, Granny?"

"Under my bed, close to the edge so I can grab it, if necessary."

"Okay." She went upstairs to put it away.

Nora hadn't seen the local news while they were at Hunting Valley. At Brian's house, they didn't carry the Youngstown area stations. Amy had brought her iPad with her. She turned it to a local news station.

As one of the side stories, the reporter mentioned the break-in. "There still has been no arrest in the case of the home invasion and hostage situation in Smith Township last week. Police are currently looking for these men for questioning." The reporter repeated the real names of Primo, Nails, and Tonto as their photos appeared side by side on Amy's iPad.

Nora shook her head. "I wonder if they'll ever be caught. Maybe all three of them went to Mexico."

Amy suggested, "Give it some time. It's only been a week since they escaped."

"You're right. I need to be patient. But it's so frustrating. And they haven't found any of my things yet either. I guess I have to be thankful they haven't tried to transfer my stocks yet. I called my broker while at Brian's house."

"See, at least something is promising."

Nora puckered her lips. "I guess. I know those guys were career criminals and probably had countless connections the police didn't know about. I just have to be patient and bide my time. That's all."

Chapter Twenty-Three

Very Early Saturday Morning

Since Sonya had taken over Amy's old bedroom, Amy slept in the guest room that Friday night. Nora took a very hot and lengthy shower before slipping into her pajamas. It was nice being at Brian's, but she was glad to be home to somewhat a semblance of order and familiarity. However, she realized, she'd need to find a new normal and familiar order now that Dave was gone and her life had been turned up-side-down. She'd also have to put that wretched ordeal behind her and completely out of her mind.

While lying in bed trying to sleep, Nora's mind went on a roller coaster of memories, mostly about Dave, but also their kids and grandkids. As they were good memories, she actually welcomed their intrusion into her mind.

She wasn't sure what time she eventually fell asleep. Probably sometime around one-thirty or two. What she was sure of was the sound she heard of glass breaking about three o'clock and suddenly awakening her. She didn't stop to think or second-guess herself. Instantly alert, she jumped out of bed, quietly ran into the bathroom and grabbed her revolver from the panty liner box.

Whatever the noise was, this time she'd be

prepared for anything. She rushed back to the bedroom and grabbed the iron pipe from under the bed. All three dogs were on all fours with their hair standing straight up along the middle of their backs. Low growls came from Amos and Cleo.

She crept silently into the hall. Amy was tentatively walking out of the guest room with her hair disheveled and a bewildered cloud over her face. Looking at Nora, she shrugged her shoulders.

Nora's bedroom was on one side of the staircase. The other three rooms were on the opposite side. She whispered across the top of the stairs to Amy. "Close and lock the kids' doors. The scumbags are back." Then Nora handed her the iron pipe before Amy hurried to close the kids' doors.

She took the safety off the Smith & Wesson and put her finger on the trigger, pointing the gun toward the floor. She would be ready for them this time. Amy returned and took a position on the opposite side of the staircase with the iron pipe raised in her hand. They waited.

The downstairs intruders took their good old time moving around. They should've known that old bitch was not some feeble invalid who couldn't see or hear anymore. For a sixty-six-year-old woman, Nora had pretty good hearing. Since she had her cataracts removed two years ago, her eyesight wasn't so bad either. Most important, if needed, she knew she could fire her gun. Those scumbags should've known that.

She finally heard the shuffle of feet on the carpet approaching the staircase. They were stepping very lightly, perhaps figuring she was sound asleep in her comfortable bed. No chance of that.

Since she and Amy were hugging the wall at the top of the stairs away from the view of anyone approaching them, Nora could sense when they began to climb the first step. She was aware they might have their guns drawn, so she couldn't waste a millisecond. She nodded her head to Amy. Amy nodded in return.

Then it happened.

Primo was the first to approach the top of the stairs. As soon as his body inched into her view, Nora shot him, and Amy bashed him in the head. He immediately fell partly on the landing, his body instantly motionless.

Wasting no time, Nora put the front of her body against the wall, pointed her right arm down the stairs, and blindly fired over Primo's fallen form until the gun was empty. She stood against the wall breathing heavily for a few seconds, waiting to hear any sounds from down the staircase.

Cries and moans erupted from below, but she heard no footsteps. Since her gun was empty, she was afraid to look around the corner. It wasn't necessary. In the next second, Amos and Cleo bounded down the hall, trampled over Primo's body, and ran down the stairs. Only then did she chance to peek around the corner.

Both men were lying still. Nails on the last few steps, his head resting on Primo's feet. Tonto on the hall floor below. The sounds of agony were coming from him. Amos was biting Nails' ear while Cleo was atop Tonto's back, sinking her teeth into his fleshy cheek. The dogs were howling and growling incessantly.

"Amy, call 9-1-1!"

Amy ran back into the guest room, grabbed her phone, and dialed the number while the dogs kept snarling and attacking the men. At that point, the kids pounded on their bedroom doors, screaming to get out.

Primo did not move. Nora picked up the gun he had dropped and pointed it down the stairs. She screamed at the dogs, "Amos! Cleo! Stop!"

Moving their muzzles back and forth, the dogs smelled their captives for a few seconds more before jumping off them. All hyped up, they scrambled and paced around the hallway for several seconds before stopping and panting.

Gordy had been barking the entire time the shooting was occurring. He finally took a position beside Nora and pranced nervously.

Amy had unlocked the kids' doors, and they rushed toward Nora. They both stopped suddenly at the staircase. Collin's mouth opened wide enough to slide in a grapefruit, and his eyes looked like two hard-boiled eggs with big spots in the middle. Sonya screamed and covered her mouth.

The four of them and Gordy stood silently at the top of the stairs, probably in shock. The two dogs downstairs kept pacing in circles. When at last Nora heard the sirens, she shook her head to focus again on what she had to do. Out of breath and breathing heavily, she panted, "I have to unlock the door for the police."

Collin interrupted. "Let me do it, Granny. It'll be easier for me to get down the steps."

Nora looked over at Amy, questioning if this was okay with her. Amy responded, "Let him do it. He's right. You might trip with those knees of yours."

Railings were on both sides of the staircase. Using them, Collin, skipped and hurled his supple frame through the maze of blood and bodies. He made it to the hallway below just as the pounding began on the front door. Within seconds, the front door opened and the noise of a rush of activity echoed up the staircase.

The three at the top of the stairs stared down as a half dozen policemen came into their view. One of the officers said, "Oh, my God. This is a bloodbath!"

Nora still held Primo's gun down to her side. Another officer yelled, "Drop your weapon, ma'am."

Nora gently placed the gun on the hall carpet.

Chapter Twenty-Four

Decisions and Reflections

They had to remove the bodies before Nora, Amy, and Sonya could get downstairs to give their statements. Primo was dead. He died instantly when the bullet Nora shot angled into his side, traveling through his lungs and heart. Nails died in the ambulance before he reached the hospital. One of Nora's bullets had hit him in the neck. They said one also penetrated his shoulder, but the shot in the neck was what killed him. Tonto was alive but in very serious condition. The bullet that had gone through Nails' neck had also hit Tonto in the face and through a portion of his brain. Nails' ear had been bitten off by Amos. It was lying on the step beside Amos' paw. As for Tonto, if he recovered, the doctors expected he would have serious brain injuries and would be unable to function normally. According to the doctors, he'd never have the ability to appear in court for his trial.

When Deet went to trial, the judge charged him with aiding and abetting in the home invasion and kidnapping. At his sentencing, he was ordered to be confined to the juvenile detention center for eighteen months after which he'd be on probation for another year. During that probationary period, he'd be required to participate in some type of community service activity. Sonya wanted nothing to do with him now. She didn't exactly hold a grudge against him but felt he no longer deserve her friendship. Forgiveness is hard sometimes.

Speaking of friendships, that expensive locket the thieves stole from among Sonya's things was given to her by Kyle. Apparently, they were more than just friends. However, Amy had told her she had to wait until she was at least sixteen to be officially dating. It was okay to go out with Kyle as long as they were in a group, but not alone. Amy was thinking back on her own mistakes when she was Sonya's age. Dave and Nora probably should've been a little stricter with Amy also. Nora always said there should be a book on how to raise children, one that really worked. She could've used it for both her children.

The front door of Nora's house had two new decorative, etched glass windows installed, one on each side of it. On the day Nora shot them, those bastards broke one of the old windows to get access into her house. At the time, no curtains or blinds adorned the windows; they were simply opaque glass. She was surprised how easily those men broke the window. The police said the invaders used a hammer that was found on the doorstep.

When those culprits came to her house the second time to kill them, all her physical property was still in Nails' black van, which he had parked in her driveway again. After a few weeks, her belongings were returned to her. Most of the money they had taken was gone or hidden somewhere. She considered that a small price to pay compared to what she could've lost.

None of this made her feel satisfied or vindicated.

She had never asked for this. She had done nothing to deserve their invasion of her property and her life. She certainly did not deserve for those men to come back a second time for the sole purpose of killing her and her family. Most of all, she didn't deserve to be left with the guilt of taking the lives of two human beings and leaving the third without any cognitive ability—even if they were assholes.

After the shooting, while some officers remained at her house with the bodies, two officers escorted Nora, Amy, and the kids to police headquarters to give their account of what happened. The dogs were temporarily taken to the Pet Paws Hotel until the CSI unit finished with the crime scene.

Nora was not charged in the deaths of Nails and Primo, or the maiming of Tonto. However, that didn't make her feel blameless or absolve her conscience. Too often she looked back and guiltily thought if she only had called the police when that black van tried to run her off the road; if she had called them when she saw a strange light in the woods behind her house; if she had called them when she noticed the mangled doggie door—if, if, if. She had done none of those things. Therefore, was all that had happened her fault? The entire fiasco was her fault? That's what Nails' girlfriend said. That's what Tonto's parents claimed. Sometimes that's what *she* thought also, for she will always hold herself responsible to some degree.

People asked her if she were glad she shot those men, killing two of them. Is that a stupid thing to ask? Maybe not. She knew she could be a bitch, but a killer she was not.

The simple answer? Nora had no choice. How did

the expression go? Kill or be killed. She was put in that situation. She was glad they could no longer hurt or threaten her family or anyone else's family, but she was so, so sorry she had to be the one to stop them. Looking back, she wished they had been captured by the police, spent their time in prison, and emerged model citizens many years later. But everybody knows everything doesn't have a fairy tale ending.

She often wondered why Primo had to be so greedy. Why didn't he just take all the things they had gathered from the house and leave her and her grandchildren alone? Dave's antique knives especially. They were priceless. Of course, she would've been upset with losing all those things, but hell, they weren't worth anybody's life. It didn't make any sense, holding the three of them captive for days. It made her think perhaps that wasn't just a home invasion. Maybe from the very beginning, they were playing some kind of twisted game. How much could they terrorize them? How much could they make them beg? What did Nora think? She thought they planned to kill them from day one, especially her, the minute they targeted her on that rainy night coming home from Zep's Pizza when they tried to run her off the road with their big, black van.

****

A couple of good things came out of all this. Nora cherishes her new relationship with Brian and Lisa. She talks to both of them at least once a week, and they now visit each other often. She only wished she had faced the reality sooner that she was the one hindering their friendship, not Brian or Lisa. She had wasted so many years.

She also became closer to Sonya and Collin. They

spent the remainder of their summer vacation with her and did loads of fun things. They are great kids, and they will be outstanding adults. Without their help, the three of them would never have survived. Amy did get them some counseling, but they'll be okay.

Amy and Carlos got back together. They were remarried with just a few people at the wedding. Sonya and Collin stood up for them. How the second marriage will turn out remains to be seen. They bought a house in Canfield off Shields Road. The kids are ecstatic about the reconciliation and their new house. Nora sincerely hopes it works out. Amy needs someone with whom to spend her life. Nora knows that more than anyone now that Dave is gone.

What about Nora? She still misses Dave with all her heart and soul. She thinks of him every day and wishes he were still here beside her. She will feel that way until the day she dies. But she has come to the realization that she can go on living and still enjoy life to some degree without him. It's hard, but she is doing it. She's joined a few senior groups to help keep her busy. She's volunteered at her church in many capacities. So she is keeping herself occupied. And she has actually started to write a book about the terrible ordeal she lived through. It is very therapeutic for her.

She has put her house on Smith Garner Road up for sale. It holds too many memories. She doesn't want to live there anymore. Granted, most of those memories were good ones. Great ones, in fact. But the strength of those horrible ones has come to outweigh the good for her. Plus, the house and the property are just too much for an old woman to maintain on her own. The place needs a family, not a tired, old widow. She is buying a smaller house off Shields Road about a mile from where Amy's family have moved. She'll have two acres, just enough for Amos, Gordy, and Cleo to enjoy. Those dogs still give her great comfort. But they too won't last forever.

Collin says he'll mow the lawn for her at her new place, and Sonya says she'll help her with the landscaping. Nora feels good about it and is getting anxious to rid herself of this place and work in her new garden.

Right now, Nora sits on the living room couch, sipping a cup of Earl Grey tea and eating a snickerdoodle cookie she baked this morning. At intervals, she places the cup on the end table and puts the cookie down on the small plate. Gordy is at her side, turning and turning to get comfortable. Nothing new with that. Amos and Cleo are both at her feet. Amos is lightly snoring. It's a comforting sound. Cleo still misses Dave. She's getting better, but sometimes she still searches for him before coming back to Nora. Maybe Cleo won't search any more in the new house.

It's a hot, sunny day outside. The wings of her metal butterflies on the sculpture in her flower garden are gently moving in the light breeze. The flowers are changing from late spring flowers to late summer beauties. She watered them earlier that day.

Oh, there's the red cardinal again! And there's his brown mate. Lucky, lucky birds.

A word about the author...

When you are young, you have hopes, dreams, and even schemes about what path you will take in life. I was positive I would become a commercial artist. When that didn't happen, I became an art teacher. After five years, circumstances made that career no longer an option, and I became a staff accountant for a CPA firm. During this "path", my daughter and I took an unexpected detour and established a non-profit animal shelter for abandoned and abused animals. Because we needed funds to support our increasing animal family, we wrote a book, Let Freedom Ring, hoping it would be a best seller. The book received good ratings but never made any best seller lists or helped much with our financial needs.

Then my life's path encountered a very deep hole and took an abrupt and devastating change of direction. My daughter passed away from breast cancer, and I had to find appropriate homes for all our animals. When that overwhelming task was completed, I remained at my accounting position until I retired because my failing eyesight became a major problem.

As you can see, my life's path took many twists and turns along the way. I now spend my retirement years writing manuscripts that I hope become published books. There Was an Old Woman is my fifth published mystery/thriller. Not too bad for an eighty-year-old woman, right? The other books also received good reviews but were also never on any best seller list. Maybe this one will make it.

Thank you for purchasing
this publication of The Wild Rose Press, Inc.

For questions or more information
contact us at
info@thewildrosepress.com.

The Wild Rose Press, Inc.
www.thewildrosepress.com